Bad Hair Day

Bad Hair Day

• • •

Adrienne Vincent Sutton

NOVEL HOUSE

Novel House
ISBN: 9780990498407
ISBN: 0990498409

adriennevincentsutton.com

For Levon, Simone, Charlotte, Mom and Dad.

One

"The thing about going to a black church is, you're going to be there all day long," I whispered to Hannah.

"Gabby!" Mom said. "That's not true."

"Sure it is, Eva," Ma McGee said, chuckling. "And since we'll be there all day, we don't need to hurt ourselves tryin' to get there. Lord have mercy, slow down Gabby!"

Mom rolled her eyes. It was a nice but chilly March morning, and Mom, Ma McGee (my grandmother), my friend Hannah, and I were all taking the short walk from our house to Reed Street Baptist Church for the eleven o'clock service. And even though Ma McGee wanted to take her time, we were late—really late. Which, I guess, was kind of my fault. Or was it Ma McGee's? Either way, we needed to pick up the pace so we wouldn't miss Dad's sermon, or even more important, so my hair would still look decent by the time we got there. The air was misty, and I swear I could feel the little corkscrew curls I had in the front starting to frizz up. I had already survived one potential hair disaster this morning that took Ma McGee *forever* to fix, and I didn't need another—especially not today.

I looked over at Mom. She gave me one of her "not now" looks, which I returned with an "I'm sorry" wince. OK, I'll admit my "all day long" estimate wasn't true, but it sure felt like it, and I'm an expert. My dad is the pastor at Reed Street, and we practically live there. Sunday is morning service, Tuesday is Bible study, Wednesday is prayer meeting, Friday is youth night, and Saturday is soup kitchen. Plus, Dad gets invited to be a guest preacher a lot, so I've been to almost every church within two hours of my house. Trust me, when it comes to churches—black, white, Baptist, Presbyterian, or whatever—I know my stuff. And even though I know that Mom is tired of me complaining about how long church is, I thought it was only fair that, as our guest, Hannah was prepared. See, Hannah had never been to a black church before. She just happens to be white—like about 99.99 percent of all the kids at our snooty, ultra-private school, Thornton Prep. Well, there aren't *that* many white kids, but it sure seems that way sometimes, and I seriously doubt any of them know what it's like to sit through three to four hours of hymns, announcements, alter calls, and preaching.

As we walked the familiar route, I noticed that a certain blue house with white trim had all its lights off and that one car was missing from its parking spot. Looks like Evonne may have been right when she called to give me the heads up about a "special visitor" coming today. Was it wrong that I was more excited about seeing *him* than listening to Dad's sermon?

When we rounded the corner toward the church parking lot, we saw that there would be *lots* of visitors today. Reed Street was packed! It looked like most of the town of Lofton was there.

As we entered the church lobby, a smiling usher handing out programs said, "Good morning, Mrs. McGee."

"Good morning," Mom and Ma McGee replied in unison.

I stifled a giggle. I don't know if Ma McGee will ever get used to the fact that Mom is the First Lady of Reed Street now. Even though it's been, like, three years since Grandpa passed and Dad took over, she's still at every church function and walks in on Sundays like she's the Queen Bee.

After quickly and quietly entering the church sanctuary, we took our usual pew up front, and I did my best to scan the room without looking like I was scanning the room. As the choir repeated the chorus of "We've Come This Far By Faith" for the hundredth time, men, women, and children dressed head to toe in their Sunday best nodded their heads to the beat. The deacon and deaconess boards held court in the front pews, and Mrs. Henry—a Reed Street regular— held up the collection plate, trying to get change back from a five-dollar bill. Packed pews aside, it was shaping up to be a typical Sunday, which meant the prediction I'd given Hannah was coming true. We'd arrived an hour late and Dad hadn't even started his sermon yet.

Most people in Lofton know my dad, so that means most people know me as "Pastor Robert McGee's daughter" which can be really annoying. Don't get me wrong, I'm real proud of my dad. Especially on days like Easter and Christmas when the church is packed and all eyes are on him. It's kind of like he's a celebrity. Not that he's stalked by the paparazzi or anything, but people do make a fuss over him. They really go on and on about how much they love his sermons and how much he means to them. But it can be really awkward for me. These days I just try to blend in with everyone else, and it hasn't been easy. From my hair right down to my shoes, I look like the "before" picture on one of those reality make-over shows—five feet and two inches of bad hair and nerdy clothes. Finally, Dad approached the pulpit and began.

"Today's sermon topic is a question: What are you so afraid of?" Dad said. "Again, I ask: What are you so afraid of? God is there. He is always there . . . to show you the way . . . if you let him."

The congregation was really feeling it.

"*Mm-hmm.*"

"*Amen!*"

"*Wellllll.*"

"*Preach, Pastor McGee!*"

"It may not be the way you want to go or even think you can tread," Dad continued. "But if you trust in him, you can."

I shifted in the pew, fiddled with my corkscrew curls, and glanced at Hannah. She looked great in a black sweater mini dress, black tights, and knee-high boots. Plus, her matching headband held every single strand of her long golden-blond hair perfectly in place. She was the ultimate picture of casual and chic. Unfortunately, next to her I looked formal and foolish in a calf-length pink dress with matching cardigan. But at least Hannah seemed to be enjoying herself. Actually, she was really getting into it, clapping and shouting in all the right places. I, on the other hand, had spent most of Dad's sermon worrying about how my hair was holding up. I guess I felt like I could take a pass on listening that day. Today's sermon sounded a lot like the lecture Dad gave me last week after I told him I might be stuck in the seventh grade forever because math just isn't my thing.

In fact, the future I imagine doesn't have a single plus, minus, or equal sign in it. I plan on creating a culinary empire that will give Martha Stewart and Rachael Ray some serious competition. But before doing any of that, I felt like I *had* to do something about my hair.

See, my mom has seen fit to leave my hair in its natural state. Which would be fine if I had "good hair." Unfortunately, I have some of the coarsest, thickest—and I'll just say it—nappiest hair known to man, or at least Lofton. A year ago it wasn't too big of a deal, since most girls were still wearing cornrows and ponytails. But now it seems like everyone's getting their hair permed except me. Mom just doesn't get it. Maybe walking around with your hair sticking out all over the place is cool for adults, but whether or not you have good hair can make or break you in the middle school social scene. Not that I know that much about being social. Mom and Dad pretty much keep me on lockdown, and they've made it very clear that I can't officially date until I'm sixteen. But my best friend, Evonne, said that doesn't matter. I should at least look the part of a dateable girl, because those girls have the most fun. It even said so in this month's *Hey Girl!* magazine Top Tip Number 3: "Life without style is no life at all." Well, it's pretty hard having any style with this mess of naps on my head.

Mom says that everyone has good hair and I need to start appreciating every kink, coil, and curl I have. Doesn't she know that all boys want a girl with hair they can run their fingers through? You can't even run a comb through mine. And every day it gets more out of control. While everyone else's hair grows long and straight, mine just grows out—as in out of control. There's some hope, though. Mom says that I can get a perm when I'm old enough to pay for one. What she didn't know was that after lots of pushing from Evonne, I started saving up my allowance and I almost had enough for a trip to the salon. And I couldn't get the rest of it too soon, because I needed to get my hair game together—now.

This morning, Ma McGee fixed my hair up in two popcorn-ball ponytails with a few corkscrew curls in front that she formed with her curling iron in the front. It was cute—better than how Mom did it—but I looked kind of like Minnie Mouse, which was definitely not the look I was going for. Most guys described the girls they wanted to talk to as "fine" or "bangin." Minnie, as cute as she is, is neither of those. But I had high hopes that my naps would soon be a distant memory.

Anyway, in between daydreaming and stressing about my hair, I finally spied my "special visitor," AKA my crush, Mason Gambrell! Evonne's heads-up about him coming today was right. I see him around the neighborhood all the time, but I'd never seen him in church before. Mason goes to Lofton Middle with Evonne and all the other kids in Lofton except me. I *was* going to public school along with everyone else until fifth grade. Now I go to this corny private school called Thornton Preparatory Academy. Mom graduated from Thornton back in the day, and she's convinced it started her on the path to being a lawyer. I thought she'd change her mind about me going, but she wouldn't budge. Dad tried to help. I mean, look at how he turned out. He's the pastor of a church! But maybe if Dad had talked more about Lofton's classes and less about their basketball team, I could see Mason every day instead of hearing about him from Evonne.

Mason is a grade older than me—an eighth-grade star forward on the Lofton Middle School basketball team. Mason's so good that high school coaches are scouting him. And, according to Evonne—my best source for all the gossip at Lofton Middle—most of the girls at school are after him too. The scoop was that Mason used to date some girl at another school, but they just broke up and now girls were falling all over themselves to be next in line. Evonne said girls were leaving him notes and following him in the halls—and that he even had his own little cheering section at every game. I couldn't be *that* bold, but I wished I could at least have a normal conversation with him. Unfortunately, the thought of having anything to do with Mason made my stomach do backflips, and I couldn't think of anything to say. Still, as I sat in the pew, I silently thanked God that Ma McGee had redone my hair that morning.

"This don't make no kinda sense Eva," she said to Mom as she parted my hair at the kitchen table. "If you're not going to let this child get a perm—which, Lord knows, I still don't understand—you should at least learn how to do her hair right."

Mom shot Dad a look, which he ignored by burying his head in his paper and stuffing a big forkful of the buttermilk pancakes I'd made into his mouth. He wasn't about to get in between them, so Ma McGee just kept fussing.

"Looks like Stevie Wonder did this," she said, frowning. "I guess cookin' *and* doin' hair done skipped a generation."

I tried my best not to laugh, Dad got busy with a sausage link, and Mom walked out of the kitchen. She would never admit it, but Ma McGee was right: Mom couldn't cook or do hair. Ma McGee used to complain all the time about how all of her prized homemade recipes would waste away since she only had sons who wanted to eat and not cook, and a daughter-in-law who "couldn't boil water." So about two years ago, she taught me everything she knew. At first, I wasn't feeling it AT ALL. Even though Mom and Dad made sure I had no life, I could *daydream* of better things to do than to spend my spare time slaving away in the kitchen. Plus, how old school is that? Having your grandmother teach you how to cook? Would sewing and needlepoint be next? Well, fortunately, Ma McGee caught me at a weak point one day when we went over her house to visit. I was starving, and she lured me into her kitchen with promises of fried chicken, mac 'n' cheese, homemade yeast rolls, and a triple-layer chocolate cake—if I would only help her out a little. It turned out that we had the best time creating one of the best meals I'd ever tasted.

Now, I never miss the chance to cook with Ma McGee. She mostly makes soul food and Southern dishes, which I quickly mastered. But before long, with the help of the Internet and the Food Network, I was trying my hand at Italian, French, and Asian cuisines all on my own. In fact, I went kind of nuts over it. I get excited about the way flavors come together. I'm wild about the blend of salty and sweet in my candied bacon. I get psyched when I make perfect char marks on a juicy grilled steak. And I love finding funky flavor combinations like dark chocolate and parmesan cheese. I guess it's kind of weird for a twelve-year-old to be just as excited about cooking as they are about the latest pop star, but I love it.

Unfortunately, I didn't pick up Ma McGee's hairstyling skills. I was as bad as Mom, probably worse because I had no clue where to start. Even after searching hundreds of blogs and YouTube videos, my tries at the cool hairstyles I saw were a joke. I only lucked out this Sunday because Ma McGee came by our house early to have breakfast with us before church. She took one look at me and insisted on doing my hair. There was no way she would have her baby going to church looking like "who did what to who."

So, for a change, Mason didn't see me in one of my mom's jacked-up hairstyles. And he looked different, too. I was used to seeing him in jeans or basketball sweats, but of course today he was in a suit and tie looking better than ever. His suit actually made him look a little less skinny. Not that I cared. Skinny or not, this boy was beyond fine.

I tried to focus on church but it was tough. Watching Mason, daydreaming, and worrying about my hair . . . all while Mom—who Evonne called Warden Number 1—kept one eye on me at all times and Dad, aka Warden Number 2, delivered the Word.

I was also highly aware of the nasty looks Leela and her crew were sending me from three rows back. Like Mason and Evonne, Leela was from my neighborhood. Only she didn't seem to like me, and I had no idea why. Mom said that's just the way kids are sometimes, and it's a roller coaster. One minute they hate you, and the next minute they're your best friend. In fact, she thinks Leela is probably jealous of me. Yeah, right. The head cheerleader with the perfect hair was just dying to be like the preacher's daughter, who, on her best day, looked like Minnie Mouse. Nope. Leela was probably giving me the stink eye because

Hannah was with me. Looking around, I guess Hannah did stand out. The church was filled with black folks singing and shouting "Hallelujah," and there sat one smiling white girl in the front, next to the pastor's daughter.

Whatever. I had just started hanging out with Hannah, but she's real cool. Well, she is *now*. Up until a few weeks ago, Hannah was a member of Thornton Prep's Snob Mob. They're kind of like Leela and her crew at Lofton Middle but with money. I can't stand them, but even I have to admit, they have it all. Camille—head of the mob and the only black girl to break into Thornton's inner circle—was beautiful and popular, got straight A's, and her parents gave her anything she wanted. And if that wasn't enough, she was seeing one of the cutest guys in school, Derek Arrington, who was pretty high up on the Thornton Prep food chain himself. Like Camille, he got straight A's and his parents were loaded. But, unlike Camille, he had all that and still managed to be a nice person. Then again, being rich is all new to him. Derek used to go to Lofton Middle up until last year and even *I* had more than him. Every once in a while I'd even see his mom picking up some of the free groceries they handed out at Reed Street, and sometimes his dad did odd jobs for the church administrator. None of that mattered to Evonne though. She had a crush on Derek and was working up the nerve to tell him, but before she could, his dad won the state lottery jackpot—23.7 million dollars! After that, his family packed up and moved to Rodgers Park, where Hannah, Camille, and most of the other rich kids that go to Thornton live. Camille immediately went after him.

"He's way out of my league now," Evonne said after hearing he was transferring to Thornton.

"Come on, Derek is still Derek," I argued.

"Girl, did you see the new ride that his mom drives him around in?" she said. "A pimped-out Mercedes SUV! He used to *walk* to school."

"Well, of course they're going to get new stuff, Evonne," I said. "That doesn't mean he's better than us. He'd be lucky to hang with a girl like you."

Evonne smiled. "Thanks Gab, but I can't compete with Camille."

And, although I hated to admit it, it was kind of true. I mean Evonne's my girl and she's cute and all, but I think that even she would admit (after being hung upside down and tortured) that Camille is beautiful. Actually, she's gorgeous. She has perfect brown skin, hazel eyes that are kind of hard not to stare at, and hair that's straight, thick, and falls to the middle of her back. It's the kind of hair that you can do *anything* with. She had it cut into a super-cute bob at the beginning of the year, and I swear it grew back to the middle of her back in two months like she was Rapunzel or something.

"Yeah, well, she's still not as great as she thinks she is," I countered. "She swears she's the queen of Thornton Prep."

"You mean like Hannah?"

Evonne didn't trust Hannah and had warned me to stay away from her, but Hannah's cool. After quitting the Snob Mob, she asked me about a homework assignment one day during lunch and we became fast friends. Hannah said that being friends with Camille was "too exhausting."

I didn't really think about Hannah being white *except* when she started asking me all kinds of questions about black people. Which was funny, because I didn't feel like I knew any more than she did. Plus, even though I've known most of the kids at Lofton Middle since elementary school, in some ways, Hannah had more in common with them than I did. They got to listen to rap music, hang out at the mall without their parents, and go out on dates. The girls have names like Leela or Jordan, hair that *always* looked perfect, and clothes like the celebrities you see in the pages of *Hey Girl!* and *Teen Vogue*. And then there's me. When I wasn't wearing a school uniform, I was a walking advertisement for the very latest in nerd-girl fashion from my mom's favorite store, Jane's Juniors. Plus, a big night out for me is a parent-approved movie and pizza with my folks. I've been kind of OK with it all up until now, but this year, things feel different. It's like there's this party that everyone's been invited to except me, and—for the very first time—I really, *really*, want an invitation.

Suddenly, Hannah tapped me on my knee, jerking me out of my thoughts and back into the sanctuary. She had a "What's going on?" look as my dad approached the pulpit again.

"He's just giving the benediction," I whispered. "That means it's time to go." She breathed a sigh of relief, and I chuckled. Even though she seemed to enjoy the service, I know that there was only so much she could take.

Once my dad, the ministerial staff, and the choir had walked down the aisle and out the door, folks started heading out. Dad signaled for Mom, Hannah, and me to come to him as he greeted the people leaving. As we made our way outside of the sanctuary, I could see he was talking to Mason and his folks.

"He's cute," whispered Hannah.

Suddenly, I wished Evonne was here instead of Hannah. Evonne was cool in a crisis and she knew how to calm me down. Unfortunately, Evonne and her mom were members of Bedside Baptist, aka Pillow Presbyterian, aka Church of the Holy Comforter. She was probably snoring like a rhino right now.

"Actually, Mason isn't much older than Gabby and Hannah," my father told Mason's parents as we walked up. I reached for my stomach. More backflips!

"Hey, Gabby, you know the Gambrells," Dad said.

My lips seemed to be stuck together, so I just nodded.

"This is Gabby's classmate, Hannah," he continued.

Even though I saw Mason around in the neighborhood, I'd never really talked to him except for a quick "Hey." Today, he was on my turf, but I was still a mess. It felt like the temperature had suddenly reached 100 degrees, I was wearing ten sweaters, and someone had stuffed my mouth with a million cotton balls.

"Mason's father and I were friends at Lofton Middle and Lofton High," Dad explained.

Looking at my dad in his preacher's robe standing next to Mr. Gambrell in his purple pinstriped suit, matching hat, and, like, a thousand rings on his hands, it was hard to imagine that they could have ever been friends.

"We even played basketball together," Dad continued. "Although, I haven't seen too much of him since then. Especially in *here*."

"Well, Rob, you know how it is," Mr. Gambrell said with a laugh. "But I figured it wouldn't hurt to come in here and send up a few extra prayers. You do know that Mason is in line to break your record next Saturday."

"Yeah, Mike, I know," Dad said. "But thanks for reminding me."

I couldn't believe it! I mean, I knew that Mason was on pace to break the single season scoring record at Lofton Middle this year. But I had no idea that it was *Dad's* record. Mason was only seven points away, and everyone thought that next Saturday would be the day he did it. They would actually be playing Thornton Prep—for the first time ever—for the chance to qualify for the state championship, and it was sure to be an easy win for Lofton. Thornton Prep wasn't exactly a basketball powerhouse and it would be no problem for Mason to score seven points or 77 for that matter.

"Actually, Gabby, back in the day, I gave your dad a run for his money with that record," Mr. Gambrell said as he shot an imaginary basketball.

"I don't quite remember it that way," Mom chimed in.

"Well, *I* do," Mrs. Gambrell said, looking slightly annoyed. "And I should know. I led the cheers at every game."

"Yeah, and what does a Thornton Prep girl know, anyway?" Mr. Gambrell teased. "Fact is, if Rob hadn't been such a ball hog, that scoring record would have been mine that year."

Mom wouldn't let it go. "I don't think—"

"Well, that's ancient history," Mr. Gambrell said. "It's Mason's turn now. So, son, do you think you can do it?"

"Of course," Mason said, high-fiving his dad.

"What I want to know is, do you think you guys will be able to win your next two games to qualify for the state championship?" Dad asked.

"We're going to straight-up embarrass whoever steps out on the court against us, Rev. McGee," Mason said, grinning.

Dad and Mr. Gambrell looked at each other, shook their heads, and laughed. I don't remember too much after that. My folks and Mason's parents started talking, and Hannah started asking Mason about basketball. Actually, she talked his head off, flipping her perfect hair, while I stood there with my sweaters and cotton balls and looking stupid. I'd remember this the next time I had the bright idea of inviting Hannah to church.

Two

"OK, Gab. I think I got it this time," Mom said, concentrating like a surgeon as she braided my hair.

It was Monday morning, and my daily torture session was in full swing as my mom tried to rake, pull, and tug my hair into submission.

"You know, this would be a whole lot easier if you would just let me get a relaxer," I said, wincing in pain. But, as usual, Mom wasn't having it.

"So all of your hair can fall out?" Mom said. "I don't think so."

"Mom, I know plenty of girls with perms, and their hair isn't falling out."

"Oh, it will, trust me."

"Well, what about braid extensions?" I asked, already knowing what she would say.

"So let me see if I understand this correctly," Mom said in a tone usually reserved for her cross-examinations. "You want me to spend three hundred dollars of my hard-earned money just so someone can put the hair of an Indian woman—who you don't even know—on your head?"

Most of the time there is no use arguing with my mom. She's always in lawyer mode, so unless what I have to say can stand up in court, I might as well let it go. Plus, Mom really gets up on her soapbox about having 100 percent, chemical-free, natural hair. It's crazy, because according to Dad, mom used to have her hair "fried, dyed, and laid to the side," courtesy of her biweekly appointment at Mrs. Henry's hair salon, Shear Wonders.

Unfortunately for me, right before I was born, she got it into her head that putting anything unnatural in or on your body was wrong. So one day she went down to Shear Wonders and told them to cut off all of her beautiful, shoulder-length, perfectly coiffed, chemically treated hair. Mrs. Henry refused, so Mom grabbed the scissors herself and started cutting off her hair right there in the salon! Well, Mrs. Henry wouldn't let her walk out of *her* shop looking all jacked up, so she finished the job by cutting Mom's hair into a very small Afro. Dad says he flipped out, but eventually he got over it. Now, she preaches to everyone she knows—including all of my friends—about the evils of perms, or "chemical fire creams," as she likes to call them. It can really be embarrassing.

All I want is hair that blows in the wind. My hair only looks good when Ma McGee does it, and that isn't too often since I don't want to hurt Mom's feelings. White girls have it easy. Hannah's hair blew in the wind and it *always* looks good. Plus, whenever she flips *her* hair around, it looks so cool—and it also feels like silk. Hannah said my hair feels crunchy. Unfortunately, she said it right in front of my mom, who gently informed Hannah that my hair was *not* crunchy. She then went on to explain that it "was richly textured, and while it didn't feel silky or move with the turn of my head, it was beautiful nonetheless." I was mortified. And, poor

Hannah, well . . . she never said another word about my hair—or anybody else's—around my mother again.

"Gabby," Mom said. "You do know that there's no such thing as 'bad hair,' right?"

"Yeah, I know, I know," I said, rolling my eyes. "You *always* tell me that."

"Hey, don't get smart," she said as she put a little more muscle into combing my hair. "I know I always tell you that, but do you *really* know it?"

I worked up my best smile and nodded.

"Look, when I was growing up, you pretty much had to have a perm," Mom said. "You were an outcast if you didn't."

Not much difference between then and now Mom, I thought.

"And even if you did have a perm," she said. "You had to make sure it was bone straight. I mean, as soon as any so-called naps showed, I was either reaching for the straightening comb or the Dark and Lovely, Dudley's, or whatever perm you could find on sale at the drugstore. I can't believe my hair didn't fall out. I'm so glad that these days more and more people are going natural."

Did my mom even watch TV? And what was Dudley's?

"You like my hair, don't you?" Mom said, smiling.

"Sure, Mom," I lied.

That day my mom's hair was in an Afro puff. I guess it was OK, but it didn't have that fresh-from-the-salon look. What I mean is, her hair wasn't all the way laid down, and it was kind of, well . . . fuzzy. Little hairs stuck out all over. I know this girl at church—Vanessa Wallace—who wears her hair in an Afro puff, too, but every hair on her head stays in place and her puff is fluffy and curly. But *she* has a relaxer. Plus, I don't really think the Afro puff is her real hair. Anyway, Mom's hair—and my mine, too—would look a lot better if she would just let somebody else style it. Unfortunately she swore off hairdressers after coming home from an appointment at Shear Wonders, ranting about "too much money, too much waiting, and not enough customer service." From then on she committed herself to learning how to do our hair herself—no matter how long it took or how bad it looked.

"Look, Gabby, bottom line: I'm not paying for a perm, extensions, or anything unnatural in your hair," Mom said.

OK, end of hair conversation.

After Mom finished, I checked my dresser mirror. Frowning, I saw that her skills hadn't improved. It was like anything that could have gone wrong went wrong—on my head. When I turned around, I saw her waiting for my approval.

"It's getting . . . better," I lied.

"Really? I thought it looked a little off again. Oh, well, I guess kids are wearing their hair different these days," she said. "Well, I need to get ready myself, so I'll see you downstairs."

I beat my mom downstairs, so I grabbed my favorite hat, headed outside, and waited for her at the corner of our lawn, which was also the school bus stop for the kids in my neighborhood. It felt more like May than March, but I still put my backpack down so I could quickly put my hat on. It was one of those oversized multicolored Rasta beanies that would have looked cool with jeans and a cute sweater. But paired with my Thornton uniform— white oxford, maroon vest, pleated shirt, and white knee socks—it looked pretty ridiculous. I didn't care. Having anyone see me without it would have been worse. As I threw my backpack over my shoulder, I noticed Evonne approaching.

"Hey, girl, what's going on?" Evonne said, eyeing my hat.

"Nothing much," I said with a sigh. "Just waiting for Warden Number 1."

Evonne chuckled. "She jacked up your hair again, huh."

"Yup."

"And, it's still 'no way' on the perm, right?"

"Uh-huh," I said, envying her freshly permed hair shining in the sun.

"I told you, you're just going to have to take matters into your own hands."

"Yeah, I guess," I said.

Evonne could see that I wasn't in the mood to discuss my hair saga for the millionth time, so she switched gears.

"So is Derek still hanging out with the Snob Mob queen?" she asked.

She knew the answer, but I nodded a sympathetic "yes." If Thornton gave out the titles Mr. and Ms. Thornton Prep, they'd have to go to Derek and Camille. Derek was class president and captain of everything from the chess club to the soccer team, and Camille was our resident "It girl." Every once in a while, Evonne would torture herself by inquiring about their status. She would get her hopes up that he'd come to his senses only to be disappointed when I reported that Camille still had Derek wrapped around her little finger.

"I haven't seen them together much lately, though," I said. "He really hasn't been in school at all in the past month. Just a day here and there. There's a rumor that something's going on with his family, but I'm not sure what, and Camille isn't saying a word."

"Not even on her blog?" Evonne asked.

I rolled my eyes. CamilleSays.com was supposed to be Camille's celebrity news/fashion/opinion blog with access for only Thornton Prep students through our school e-mail accounts. Kids read it like it was the daily news, mostly for Camille's daily "Guess Who?"—a blind item on a Thornton student who'd made a fool of themselves in some way. Unfortunately, me and my hair made "Guess Who?" a lot.

"Sorry, I guess not," Evonne said. "Well, I hope everything's OK."

"Well, whatever's going on, I'm sure I'll find out soon. Thornton's gossip network is pretty strong even without Camille's help."

"Well, let me know, OK?"

"Of course," I agreed.

"OK, enough about that. It's time for a *Jill Jones* update," Evonne said. "Is everything still set?"

"Yup!" I said.

I still couldn't believe it. We were actually going to see and maybe even meet Jasmine Jeffers, aka Jill Jones of *Jill Jones: Girl Detective*. It was our favorite show. Every Saturday night at nine o'clock, Evonne and I watched together—on the couch or over the phone—as Jill solved crimes committed by the locals of Oak Hills. Each week Jill managed to get out of tough fixes and find the bad guys. Plus she looked great doing it. Talk about good hair! It moved when she did and looked perfect, regardless of whatever crazy situation she found herself in. A few weeks ago my mom found out that they would be taping a few scenes of the show in one of the courtrooms where she works, and some of the court staff and prosecutors—including her—were invited to watch and bring guests.

"Yeah, well, I want to look *good*," Evonne said while patting down her hair. "You never know who might be there. I could get discovered."

"Yeah, right," I said, giggling. She *was* right, though. Not that we'd get discovered, but you never know who might be there. Jill Jeffers was dating Dondré Howard, one of the hottest R&B singers out right now. I read in *Hey, Girl!* that Dondré's wild about her hair and said he could spend hours playing with it. I made the mistake of showing Mom the article, thinking she might understand. She said it was one of the most ridiculous things she'd ever read. But for me, ridiculous was what was going on underneath my hat. I could feel another "Guess Who?" coming up in my future.

"Are you going to the big game next week?" Evonne asked, switching gears again.

"Yeah," I said. "With my usual escort."

"Your dad's coming *again*?"

"Yup," I said, rolling my eyes.

Lofton Middle's basketball team was really doing it this year. So far they had a winning record and needed to win just one more game to guarantee a spot in the state tournament. I should have been rooting for Thornton Prep, but I felt like Lofton was my real team. I live in Lofton and know most of the kids at the school. Plus, I *would* be going there right now if Dad could have been just a little more convincing with Mom. She wasn't really trying to hear him, though. To her, Thornton meant guaranteed success. It's weird. Mom is pretty down to earth, and you'd never guess she'd want to be around a bunch of snobs from Thornton. Anyway, since Dad was on the team back in the day, he loves to go to every game. He also likes keeping an eye on me.

"Forget your dad," Evonne said. "The important thing is you'll get to see your boy."

I grinned. Of course the game would be all about Mason. Everyone said he was a guaranteed future NBA star. He was fast. He was smooth. He was . . . coming this way!

I started to panic as we spied Mason walking up the street. I was excited to see him, but my mouth was dry, my armpits were wet and those cotton balls and sweaters were back. What was taking my mom so long? I watched as Mason traveled the sidewalk in long strides with his crew Tommy and DaShawn, who each had to take two steps to his one just to keep up.

"When I make it to the pros, I'm gonna have five houses and ten cars," Mason said as they approached.

"Me, too," DaShawn said. "Plus, I'll have crazy clothes. And no repeats. A different outfit for every day of the year."

"Yeah, well, you're gonna need a jump shot first," joked Mason while slapping five with Tommy.

"Real funny, man," DaShawn said.

When they reached the corner, Mason looked at us and offered a "What's up?"

"Hey . . . OK . . . well, I guess I'll see you guys later," I spat out, turning toward our car.

"Why? Your mom hasn't come down yet," Evonne said without missing a beat.

Trapped! Now what? Evonne stayed quiet so I could have my chance with Mason. What a friend. She was killing me! Awkward silence filled the air as I struggled with my backpack. All of sudden, it felt like it weighed a ton! Then Tommy and DaShawn started whispering. Was my hair peeking out of my hat? I reached for my head. Whew! Still covered. Then they started whistling. We all turned to see that Leela, Kameira, and Janelle were walking toward the corner. I should have known Tommy and DaShawn weren't even thinking about me. Lofton Middle's official cool clique had arrived. They had the best clothes, the best hair, and the best, well, everything. Leela, or "Lee-Lee" as she preferred to be called, ignored us and headed straight for Mason with her perfect makeup, clothes, and, of course, *hair*.

"Hey, Mase," she called.

"Hey, Lee-Lee," he answered.

"You ready to take that scoring crown next Saturday?" she asked, tossing back her shoulder-length mane.

"Of course," Mason responded, leaning in a little closer to her.

It wasn't fun watching Mason all up in Leela's face, but my heart did start beating regularly again once all the attention was off of me. Plus, you had to admire the girl. Not much fazed Leela. I would have been a mess talking to Mason, but she always had it together. Anyway, for the second time in two days, I stood there looking stupid as some other girl talked to the boy I was crazy about.

"Hey, Lee-Lee, if your folks are riding you too much about your grades, you should talk to Evonne," Mason said.

"You know she's the smartest girl at Lofton. She helped me get out of basketball suspension twice."

"Yeah, I guess," Leela said.

"Or there's Gabby," he said.

"Gabby?" she said twisting her lips.

"Yeah, she's a brain, too," he said. "You know she goes to that big-time school now. Uh, Thoreon? No Thor—"

"It's Thornton," I said, surprised to feel my mouth work.

"Oh, hi, Gabby," Leela said as she turned toward me. "I didn't even know you were there." Smirking, she said to Kameira, "Hey, isn't Gabby's hat cute?"

"Yeah," Kameira said, doing a poor job of hiding her laughter.

"Hey, let me try it on," she said, reaching for my head. I dodged her with the skill of a boxer. I wasn't about to let her reveal the hot mess underneath.

I felt my face getting hot, but—once again—I couldn't think of anything to say.

"Oh, well. You must looove that hat," Leela said. "I guess you'll be wearing it at the pre-victory party next Friday?"

Leela knew my hair was probably looking crazy under my hat *and* that I couldn't go to Lofton's pre-victory party—an event concocted by Leela and the cheer squad to celebrate Lofton's guaranteed victory over Thornton and making it into the state tournament. Like any regular party, there would be boys, so of course that meant my folks would never go for it. Who ever heard of having a pre-victory party, anyway? Most people celebrate something *after* it happens. But then again, Leela seemed to take every opportunity to party *and* get close to Mason. I'm sure she was planning a post-victory party, too.

Evonne looked like she was ready to go off on Leela, but Mason started talking before she could. "Hey, Lee-Lee, you have something in your hair."

"Ooh, where?" she said, reaching for her head.

"Wait, I'll get it," he said.

Then he retrieved the smallest piece of lint known to man from her perfectly silky, free-flowing hair.

"Thanks," she said as she smoothed down her hair.

Suddenly, I heard the words I had been waiting for since Mason had arrived.

"Gabby!" my mom called. "It's time to go."

I'd never been so happy to go to old Thornton Prep in my life.

Three

One of the nation's top 100 private schools, Thornton Preparatory Academy has a 104-year history of academic excellence, community service, and general snobbery. According to the school's pamphlet, "Thornton's campus sits on twelve perfectly landscaped acres of land, which rests in the heart of the prestigious Rodgers Park community of Lofton and boasts an administrative building, three libraries, an art gallery, a music center, a theater, and a state-of-the-art technology lab." The pamphlet doesn't lie. Thornton's only about twenty minutes from Lofton Middle, but it feels like another world.

Mom was one of the first few black students to attend, and that happened only *after* William Thornton III's very liberal great great-granddaughter threatened to pull her family's funding unless they changed the school's enrollment policies. Since she's the sole heir, they had to accommodate her "request." So now there are a few more black and brown faces in the crowd, but I still don't quite fit the mold. My Afro puffs and braids are very different from the Thornton image. Most of the teachers are used to it now, but it kills me that when my algebra teacher Mrs. Poole talks to me, she always looks at my hair instead of my face.

But that's probably because my hairdo always looks like a hair *don't.*

As I made my way to second period that Monday morning, I was being seriously harassed by Hannah. I was already a little cranky about the scene at the bus stop *and* about our art teacher, Mr. Ryan, reminding me to ditch my hat so I wouldn't violate the school dress code. Now Hannah—who was just a little too excited about the Lofton-Thornton game—was giving me a hard time about supporting Thornton. And, on top of all that, we were running late and had to move fast if we were going to make it from the first floor to the fourth.

"That gym is going to be packed with Lofton fans, so a bunch of us plan to sit together wearing our school colors," Hannah said as she darted in and out of the noisy crowd in the stairwell.

"You don't really think Thornton has a chance of winning, do you?" I asked, trying to keep up.

"Yeah, why not?"

"You met Mason," I reminded her. "He can outplay every guy on our team."

"Sure," she said. "But it takes a whole team to win, not just one guy. Our guys are getting better."

By getting better she meant that we'd won two games this year instead of one.

"You just like Steven, that's all." I said, referring to Thornton's starting point guard. I suspected that all this rah-rah stuff had less to do with school spirit and more to do with her current crush.

"Yeah, well, you like Mason," she countered. "So I guess that means you'll be rooting for Lofton.

I shrugged.

"Gee, Gabby," she said. "You should at least try to support your school."

Part of me thought she was being overly dramatic, but another part of me thought she was right. I mean, as much as I put down Thornton, I was really was lucky to be there. According to my mom, most kids who did well at Thornton Prep could write their own ticket to any college they wanted. And, as much as I hated to admit it, not all of the rich kids were snobs. Derek was really cool, and Hannah was turning out to be one of the most down-to-earth rich girls I knew. I mean, last year when she was hanging with Camille, she wouldn't have been caught dead going to church with me or attending a middle school basketball game that wasn't at Thornton. Now that she'd seen the light and ditched Queen Snob, she was preparing to sing "Onward Thornton" at the top of her lungs in the Lofton Middle School stands.

When we finally reached the fourth floor, we noticed that all the kids walking the halls were quiet and focused on their destination. Just the way Headmaster Brookfield likes it. On cue, we slowed our pace just in time before passing him as he stood right in the middle of the hall. With his tall, thin body standing perfectly straight, he looked like an English butler checking to make sure everything was in order. After nodding approvingly toward us, he resumed his watch.

"I still can't believe ole Brooksie is even letting Thornton play at Lofton's gym," I whispered.

"I know, but I don't think he had a choice," Hannah said in an equally hushed tone. "He was always coming up with excuses why we couldn't play Lofton. It was starting to look bad. I heard Thornton's granddaughter laid down the law this year."

"It's about time," I said. "Although, maybe Brooksie was trying to do us a favor. Thornton is going to get crushed next Saturday. There's no way I'm showing up in our school colors for that."

"Well, you're at least going to support the fundraising committee," she said, changing the subject. "The bake sale is next week."

"Of course," I assured her. "My cookies are your cookies."

I already had a few recipes up my sleeve. Chocolate Brownie Biscotti, Ambrosia Macaroons, and French Sablé Jammers. I'd even recruited Ma McGee as my baking assistant, and our pantry was already full of the ingredients we got last week. Although, she wasn't all that thrilled about my culinary picks.

"What's wrong with chocolate chip?" Ma McGee asked as we walked the aisles of Wickman's looking for lingonberry, apricot, and blackberry jams for my sablés.

"Nothing, except that it's the Rodgers Park community buying the cookies, not the kids," I said while inspecting a jar. "They expect something more . . . gourmet."

"Maybe," she said. "But it sounds like your mom's uppity school is rubbing off on you."

Ma McGee didn't understand. I was just serious about food and took every opportunity to expand my skills. Plus, I wasn't kidding about the people at Rodgers Park. Chocolate chip would definitely not cut it with that crowd, and Hannah agreed.

"I just hope your cookies are as fancy as you say they are," Hannah said. "We'll need the help."

The fact that we even had a Student Fundraising Committee at Thornton was ridiculous. From what I heard, Rodgers Park is filled with wealthy alumni, parents, and grandparents who make sure that the school's endowment always has enough to support whatever Thornton needs. But Mom says that the SFC makes the parents feel like their kids are learning good values by helping earn money for the school.

"So what's the cause this time?" I asked, figuring it was for another library or center we didn't need.

"Derek Arrington," she said wearily.

"Derek Arrington?"

"Yeah, I guess you didn't hear what happened."

"No, what?"

She sighed. "Derek can't afford to come to Thornton anymore."

"What? Why not? His family's rich."

"Not anymore. They've lost everything."

I stopped dead in my tracks and grabbed her arm. "What? How?"

"My mom said it was a Ponzi scheme," Hannah said.

"What's a Ponzi scheme?"

"It's some kind of phony investment scam. Anyway, I guess Camille's dad turned Derek's dad on to some big-shot investment banker who was supposed to make them a ton of money, but he ended up losing it. My dad almost got in on it, but my mom said no. She was giving my dad a bunch of 'I told you so's about it this morning."

I shook my head in disbelief. "Does that mean Camille is broke, too?" I asked, hoping that *some* good had come out of this.

"Sorry to disappoint you, but no," Hannah smirked.

I wondered why Derek's family was broke but Camille's family was fine. It would be sweet justice to see Camille having to manage without her designer clothes and cell phone. Suddenly, a delicious picture entered my head. Camille, with tattered old clothes and dirty, messed-up hair, standing in line at our church's soup kitchen and me at the door holding a bowl of soup in one hand and some of my nerdy hand-me-downs in the other.

"Derek's the one we need to worry about," Hannah said, interrupting my fantasy. "Nobody can get in touch with him. They probably already moved back to their old neighborhood."

"Wow, well, I guess he has to go back to Lofton Middle."

"Not necessarily," Hannah said with a sly grin. "This is where the SFC comes in."

"That's nice, Hannah," I said, shaking my head. "But I seriously doubt that the student fundraising committee will be able to raise enough to cover Derek's tuition next semester. What about financial aid?"

"Well, Derek's grades haven't been that great because of what his family's been going through, and I heard through the grapevine that they're looking to give his spot to the new senator's son."

My eyebrows shot up. I was always complaining about having to go to Thornton. I never knew that there were people fighting for a spot.

"So what's the plan?" I asked, knowing that a bake sale wasn't going to cover it.

Hannah told me her hope was that if she could string together enough fundraising events along with enough signatures on a "Keep Derek in School" petition, it might convince the Thornton board of directors to offer Derek a scholarship for next year.

It was nice idea—but kind of crazy when you really thought about it. Most of Thornton's students, including Hannah and Camille, had families who were rich enough to afford to send fifty students to Thornton, yet here Hannah was organizing bake sales and car washes. But Hannah knew Derek's family would *never* accept a check from her family to pay his tuition. Hopefully, her plan would work.

"Hey, I know Camille isn't into manual labor, so what's she doing to help out Derek?" I asked.

Hannah rolled her eyes. "Nothing. She broke up with him."

"What?"

"I know. I can't believe it," Hannah said.

"Well, I can," I said, fuming. "This is just like Camille. I'm just surprised it wasn't in her blog."

"Come on, Gabby. Camille's just not good with—"

"With what? Standing by a friend? Being a decent human being?" I said.

"No, what I meant is that Camille isn't good with dealing with people that are—"

"Not rich?" I said, interrupting again. "Well, that makes sense. She's never said a word to me, and I'm in most of her classes."

"Look, I'm sure Camille will come around, said Hannah. "She just has to get used to everything."

I was confused. Why was Hannah defending her? Obviously Camille had no idea about how the rest of world really lived. And she didn't want to, even though she had plenty of chances to see for herself. Even though all the kids that went to Thornton were considered rich, that wasn't the case. Sure, most students were wealthy, but there were kids that had vouchers and others (like me) who were on a partial academic scholarship. Anyway, I wasn't about to get into a debate with Hannah about Camille. She wasn't worth it.

"Well, I'd better get going," I said. "I can't afford to be late for algebra. I don't think my C-average can take it."

"Sure," she said with a laugh as she broke away to go to her own class. "See ya."

Four

Friday morning, after getting showered and dressed, I headed down the stairs into the living room with excitement and nervousness bubbling in my stomach. Today was the day. First off, not only was school closed for a teacher's conference, but it was allowance day. Every second and fourth Friday, my dad handed me a twenty-dollar bill that, after setting aside 10 percent of it for the church offering, I could use for whatever I wanted—within reason. Of course I couldn't think of anything I could do *outside* of reason with twenty dollars. Most kids even wouldn't call what I get an allowance. I mean, it didn't really "allow" me to do much of anything. Still, I always gladly accept my biweekly stipend, and for the past three months, I'd been socking most of it away into my personal "perm fund." Well, today was the day that I reached my goal of eighty-seven dollars. That's eighty dollars for a wash, cut, and perm, with seven dollars left over for a tip. Evonne told me that it was very important to tip because you didn't want them to "jack your hair all up" at your next appointment. And, if all went well, I intended to find a way to be a regular customer.

"So what's on the agenda today?" Dad asked. "Doing anything special with your allowance?"

"No, just . . . saving . . . for a rainy day," I said. "I'll be with Evonne today. I can't wait. But it's not like we're doing anything special. Just . . . hanging out . . . I guess."

Dad gave me a strange look and walked off, shaking his head.

My hands were tingling and my stomach felt like I was on the Ghoster Coaster at Riverview Park. This was going to be weird. I wasn't exactly used to lying to my folks. See, I'm the "good girl." Actually, Evonne and Hannah think I'm *too* good. I get straight A's (except for math) and never get in trouble—and where boys are concerned, well, let's just say I'm a late bloomer. Every girl I know has a boyfriend, has kissed a boy, or at the very least has been to a dance. Then there's me. I can't go to a dance until I'm thirteen or on a date until I'm sixteen—and if it were entirely up to my dad, I'd have to wait until I turned forty. Plus, usually, when given the chance to do something wrong, I can't bring myself to do it. Dad says it's because God weighs heavily on the minds of his children. I'm not so sure about that, but I do know that Mom seriously has me in check.

I mean, I love my mom, but she doesn't play. I'll never forget the first time Mom babysat my cousin Bobby.

"Bobby, I'll need you to get your foot off my table," she calmly told him after seeing him with his muddy sneaker on our glass coffee table.

We were both eight, but Bobby had been acting like a two-year-old all day—talking back, not sharing, and, in general, "standing on my mom's last nerve."

Well, when Bobby looked straight at her, and put his *other* foot on the table, I honestly thought he would die that day. After she snatched him up and took him back to her room, I ran to the door to hear his wails and screams. I really could have stayed in the living room because I'm pretty sure the whole block heard him. After what seemed like forever, he came out sniffling and rubbing his butt. Whatever Mom unleashed on Bobby worked, because he was an angel for the rest of the day. In fact, since that day, whenever he's at our house he's on his best behavior. Anyway Bobby's experience looked very painful, and my parents have expressed on more than one occasion that they agree with using this type of punishment if necessary. So I've made a personal commitment to myself *and* my behind to follow the rules. Until today.

My original plan was to present all the money I had saved up to Mom, thinking she would see how responsible and mature I was. And, since I was this responsible, mature, person, she would see how I definitely should be able to make my own choices about my hair. But Evonne didn't see it that way.

"She'll never go for it," she said last night on the phone.

"I know it won't be easy, but—"

"But nothing, Gab," Evonne said. "You know your mom is hardcore natural."

She was right, but at the same time the thought of sneaking around behind Mom's back brought up bad Bobby memories. Then Evonne brought up the scene at the bus stop. I had to admit, between seeing Mason's fingers glide through Leela's hair and being the victim of another one of my mother's failed hair experiments, I'd had enough. Really, my parents should be grateful. It's not like I'm about to run away, get arrested, or do drugs. I just want to get my hair done in a style suitable for my age. Or at least in one that doesn't look like a bad science experiment. Plus, Mom was always saying stuff like "You can't even pay for it" or "Not with my money." So, I intended to pay for it, just like she wanted.

• • •

My appointment was at Mrs. Henry's salon, Shear Wonders. Unfortunately, since she went to our church *and* Mom used to be one of her clients, she was well aware of Mom's stance on natural hair. So there was a chance that Mrs. Henry would refuse my business. But Shear Wonders was the only shop within walking distance. And, since this was a covert operation, I didn't have transportation at my disposal. Plus, the way I figured it, I probably wouldn't be turned away. Everyone knew Mrs. Henry loved money. For one thing, she *always* made change from the collection plate. And, according to my mom, she had a "no coupons, no discounts, no specials" policy at the salon. But she was so good that most people were willing to pay extra.

The walk to Shear Wonders was still kind of a hike—about two miles—but I figured the trip would be worth it to enter the land of straight, manageable hair. After milling around a bit in the house and checking the time over and over, I made myself go outside, knowing that if I didn't leave soon I'd miss my appointment. It was kind of warm, so I left without a coat, but once I'd gone too far to turn back, clouds started forming. Sure, I could have saved myself the money and hassle by plunking down $6.99 at the local beauty supply store for a home relaxer kit. But that would be like playing Russian Roulette. For every ten heads of perfectly straight hair done at home, there was a Lauren Wallace. Lauren was a classmate of Evonne's who decided to relax her own hair after her mom said she wasn't giving up any more money to hair salons. Evonne said everything started out OK, but after only a few minutes of the perm being in her hair, Lauren's scalp started burning like crazy. By the time poor Lauren had washed it out, most of her hair had washed out with it. After hearing that, I decided that if I was really going to straighten my hair, it was worth the money to have it done by a professional.

Unlike most girls, I'd never been to a hair salon before, but I'd read about plenty of them in Mom's *Essence* magazines. As soon as you walk in the door, the receptionist greets you with an offer of water, tea, juice, or some fruity adult drink while you wait. Beautiful people walk in and out of the modern salon, which is decorated with tall plants, beautiful art, and sparkling wood flooring. And before long, you're whisked away by a stylist who knows all the latest products and techniques used on all the big Hollywood stars. I couldn't wait!

I got to the salon just as it started to rain. As I opened the door, a bell rang to signal my arrival. The "receptionist" didn't look that much older than me. Still, she had lots of hair weave, a load of makeup, and the longest fingernails I'd ever seen. After waiting a few minutes for Miss Fingernails to look up from the magazine she was reading, I stated my business.

"Hi. I have a ten o'clock appointment with—"

"Aunt Angelique," she yelled toward the back with her eyes still glued to the magazine. "Your ten o'clock is here."

I stood there waiting before she finally looked up and asked, "Did you need somethin' else?"

I started to ask about my complimentary drink, but the look on her face told me that would be a mistake. As I made my way over to the waiting area, I noticed that the tall plants were plastic flowers, the beautiful art was the same collection of corny art prints I'd seen at my doctor's office, and the sparkling wood flooring was linoleum covered with balls of hair that rolled like tumbleweeds when anyone walked by. My fantasy salon had quickly faded, but I wasn't discouraged. What difference did it make what the place looked like? All I cared about was that they could do hair. And it was clear that they were experts. Each person leaving the salon looked flawless. There were a few strange styles that reached far beyond my imagination in color, length, and height, but for the most part, every person looked picture perfect. My eyes were especially drawn to the newly permed ladies. They had free-flowing hair that you could actually run your fingers through, and soon that hair would be mine!

Was there another way to get the hair I desired? Of course. Believe me, I'd already considered all of the tools of the trade black girls used to convert natural kinks into straight hair. In fact, they used all those methods at Shear Wonders. Right next to Mrs. Henry was a young stylist working lightning fast with a dryer and a huge roller brush to give a lady a blowout. Some say that the Dominican salons do it best, but don't tell that to Mrs. Henry. As far as she's concerned, Shear Wonders is the only shop in Lofton. When the stylist was done, the lady's hair was super straight, even though it looked like she was in pain.

"Girl, you really did a number on me today," she said, wincing as she looked at herself in the mirror.

The woman in the chair across from her was getting a regular flat-iron press.

The pros: You get straight hair from root to tip with a swipe of your hand. The Cons: It's only good for a week or less depending on the weather or your daily activities, not to mention the risk for neck and ear burns if you did it yourself. Then there were weaves, like the one on Miss Fingernails. An instant, pain-free solution. And, if applied correctly, there was no danger of damaging your hair. But her weave looked like it didn't belong on her head. A really good weave—one that looks like it could actually be your own hair—costs eight hundred dollars and up. Definitely not for a twelve-year-old's budget. So a relaxer seemed like the best way to go.

I sat down and started flipping though a hair magazine to pick a style. A long bob or loose curls? Parted on the left or the right? The options were endless. As I looked at the all the beautiful hair models, I chuckled at the memory of Evonne's last words to me the night before.

"Just don't go thinking you're too cute or something just 'cause you finally got them naps taken care of," she teased.

Oh, but I *was* going to look cute! I couldn't wait for the *Jill Jones* taping—and, even more important, Mason's reaction when he saw me for the first time.

After about the tenth magazine, I started to wonder if they'd forgotten about me. As I rose from my seat to check with the fingernails girl at the front desk, I looked around and noticed that there were a lot of women waiting to get their hair done but only a few stylists at work. Miss Fingernails was now chatting away on her cell phone, so

I sat back down, figuring that true beauty takes time. As the minutes turned into hours, I reasoned that true beauty must take *a lot* of time, because it was now one o'clock! Evonne was covering for me with my folks, but she could only do that until it got dark. By then my parents would be on a mission to find me *and* my behind. Finally, Mrs. Henry made her way over to me at about 2:15.

"Hey, Gabby, what you doin' here?" she asked in her heavy Jamaican accent.

I had never seen Mrs. Henry outside of church, and I almost didn't recognize her. She looked . . . well . . . rough. Mrs. Henry wasn't exactly a beauty queen, but on Sundays she was pretty put together, always wearing a dress or suit with a matching hat and heels. Today, a T-shirt and black leggings clung tightly to her heavyset frame, she was shuffling around in some old, torn house slippers and her hair was wrapped in a ratty old scarf. I had to remind myself again that appearances didn't matter. The woman could do hair.

"I'm here to get my hair done of course," I said.

"Wid out yur mudda?" she asked.

"Uh, yeah. She couldn't make it."

"Mm-hmm," she said, clearly suspicious. "OK, whut ya gettin' done today, chile? Cornrows? Plaits?"

"Actually, I want a relaxer," I said with as much confidence as I could gather.

"What?" she shrieked. "Eva's finally letting you perm dem naps?"

Mrs. Henry turned to a stylist behind her. "Connie did you here dat one? Eva's lettin' Gabby get a relaxer!" All the stylists at the salon expressed their disbelief.

"Gabby, why don't I think ur bein' totally honest wit me?" Mrs. Henry asked.

"It's true, Mrs. Henry," I lied. "My mom said that if I could pay for it, I could get it done."

"Mm-hmm," she uttered again, unconvinced.

It was time to start talking Mrs. Henry's language. And what better way to get the conversation started than by pulling out the cash that had been burning a hole in my bag all day. As Mrs. Henry's eyes danced, I knew I wouldn't have to say another word.

"Well, den, I guess when Eva sees you, *you'll* 'ave to deal wit it," Mrs. Henry said. "Let's go. I don't 'ave all day."

She couldn't wait to get her hands on my money and my hair. After I plopped down into her salon chair, she pumped it up, swiveled me around toward the mirror, and started taking out rubber bands from the ends of the crazy cornrows my mom had braided.

"Oh, chile," she said. Your hair is goin' to be *sooo* pretty. Wit all dese naps yur goin' to have some long hair."

"Really? How long?" I asked.

"'Bout down to here," she said, placing her hand about three inches down from the top of my left shoulder.

I couldn't stand it! Not only would my hair blow in the wind, but it would be longer than Leela's! I immediately pictured Mason's hand smoothing the back of my hair as we walked together. After Mrs. Henry finished looking my hair over and decided what products to use, she went in the back room to mix the relaxer. As I waited, I watched another hairdresser apply a perm to a girl a few years younger than me. A girl who looked like she was on fire! She was twisting and turning and moaning in agony. She must have been scratching her head. According to Evonne, that was a *big* mistake. If you scratched your head, the relaxer would burn your scalp like crazy and you would end up with scars and scabs. That's why after Evonne made the appointment, I didn't scratch my head at ALL. Not even when I wanted to. All of a sudden, the girl screamed out at the top of her lungs. Her mom tried her best to calm her down.

"Hold on, baby . . . just a few more minutes," her mother said. "We need to make sure it takes."

I thought she was going to combust before my eyes. She just kept twisting and turning while tears streamed down her cheeks. But I guess it was business as usual at the salon, because no one was coming to help. In fact, no one gave her a second look. It made me wonder: Just what was in that perm stuff anyway? What if I *had* scratched my head and just forgotten? And what if I ended up with tons of scabs and sores? Plus, seeing the girl with her mom, I couldn't help but think of *my* mom. I guess God can weigh on your mind anywhere. Even at Shear Wonders.

Before I knew it, I'd eased myself out of the chair and gone looking for Mrs. Henry so I could call this whole thing off. I needed more time to think this through. I knew Mrs. Henry wouldn't be happy about losing out on my money, but I figured that my conscience and my scalp would both be more than OK with my decision. As I quickly headed toward the back, the girl on fire screamed again. I turned my head back to see her and—whack! I ran right smack into the side of one of the hooded hair dryers. It immediately shut off, and I crouched down in pain. One of the dryer's sharp corners had stabbed my right side, causing a big scratch. But the woman with a head full of curlers under the dryer seemed way more concerned about the dryer than me. "Angelique!" she cried. "This girl here ran into my dryer and now I can't get this thing back on."

Mrs. Henry rushed over and started pushing buttons. "What happened?" she said.

After the lady under the dryer explained everything, Mrs. Henry turned to me. But rather than ask if I was OK, she started shouting about how I'd broken her dryer! I couldn't believe it. Now all eyes in the shop were on us as I came to my feet, and Mrs. Henry went off on me using lots of Jamaican words that I couldn't (and probably shouldn't) understand.

Finally, the lady under the dryer came to my rescue. "Angelique, I'm sure this girl didn't break your dryer."

"Yeah," another stylist chimed in. "You know that thing is as old as dirt. It was bound to go dead one of these days."

Mrs. Henry was unmoved. "All I know is, it was workin' fine, till dis one 'ere ran right into it," she cried pointing to me. "A new one gon' to cost me two hundred dollars!"

Two hundred dollars! She might as well have said two *million* dollars, because I didn't have either.

"So, little girl. How we gon' to go 'bout gettin' me my money?"

I tried to convince Mrs. Henry that I didn't break the dryer, but she wasn't hearing any of it. Everyone else in the shop shook their heads but knew there was nothing they could do to help.

"Well, we can start wit' that," she said, pointing to my purse.

I quickly fished out all the money I had, hoping it would make everything all right.

She snatched the money and counted it. "I'll get the rest from your mudda."

I went into panic mode. It was bad enough that I'd gone behind my mom's back, but now she would have to pay for a broken dryer and . . . oh, no . . . *Jill Jones*! There was no way Mom was going to let me go to the show taping now. I looked around the shop for answers and suddenly got what I thought was a brilliant idea.

"Mrs. Henry, how about letting me work off the rest of the money?" I asked.

Her eyes narrowed, but I continued.

"I could come to the salon every day after school until the dryer is paid for."

I had already invented a great story for Mom. I would tell her there was a big science project at school that Hannah and I needed to work on and we'd already started setting it up in Hannah's basement. It's amazing how fast your mind can work when you're desperate.

But Mrs. Henry wasn't hearing it. "No," she said.

"No?"

"No," she said firmly. "I don't need any more help round here."

Was she serious? Anyone looking around could see the place needed a good sweeping and dusting. Not to mention better service at the reception desk.

"I jus' want my money. Unless you got 113 dollars in the bottom of that purse, I'm going to have to call your mudda."

My desperate mind went into overdrive.

"Look Mrs. Henry, if you could just give me some more time, I'm sure I could get the rest of the money," I pleaded.

"Mm-hmm, I *knew* Eva didn't know you were down 'ere."

As I stared at the floor, that fact became even more obvious.

"OK, look 'ere," Mrs. Henry said. "If you have my money in two weeks, I won't say a word to yur mudda."

Two weeks! I opened my mouth to beg some more, but I could see that Mrs. Henry wouldn't budge.

"OK, I'll be back in two weeks," I said in defeat. Grabbing my bag, I started toward the door with no perm, no money, and no idea how I was going to raise 113 dollars.

Several ladies were waiting by the door. Their hair was done, but the rain wasn't letting up and they weren't prepared. Which was really bad for them because water on relaxed hair isn't a pretty sight. The steady rain outside would turn hair that flowed in the breeze into hair that frizzed up and didn't move. Even though I didn't have an umbrella, I walked outside without a care. The rain would have little to no effect on my natural hair. Yet another reason why I shouldn't have been there in the first place.

Five

During the second season opener of *Jill Jones: Girl Detective*, Jill had gotten herself into an impossible situation. Ignoring her curfew, she'd left her home at 1:00 a.m. to investigate the Clayton murder. Just as she discovered the clue she was looking for, Sheriff Turner caught her and, as always, did not believe her story. When the show ended, I knew that I'd find out how Jill would make things right with Sheriff Turner on next week's episode. But as I sat at the dinner table, I wasn't any closer to figuring out how to solve the fiasco that had happened earlier that day at Shear Wonders. And moving my food back and forth on my plate wasn't helping.

Most families I know hardly ever eat together. Soccer practice, dance lessons, or jobs got in the way of that. But my family isn't like most families. Even though Dad is a pastor with a needy congregation and Mom is a busy lawyer, they both make sure that they're home almost every night to eat with me. It's nice. We get a chance to talk through our day, plus Dad actually has a good sense of humor for a minister. In fact, there are lots of times that I forget that he is one. If I don't have much homework, I cook dinner. That night I made andouille sausage and shrimp gumbo with cheddar biscuits. Although it was one of my favorites, I didn't feel much like eating. This, of course, did not go unnoticed.

"What's wrong?" Mom asked as she dipped a biscuit in her gumbo.

"Nothing, I'm just not hungry," I said as thoughts of the day's events—a broken hair dryer, a furious Mrs. Henry, and a $113 debt—played like a horror movie inside my head.

Dad wasn't buying it. "The last time I checked, we don't lie in this house," he said.

If I had remembered that, I wouldn't be in this mess.

"Well, I really don't want to talk about it," I said.

"I think it could help, Gabby," Dad said, spooning the last bit of gumbo from his bowl.

"Maybe she's just having a bad hair day," Mom said. "Right, Gab?"

I nodded.

"Awww," Dad said." Your hair looks fine baby."

Well it didn't and it never did, but that's not what Mom meant. Having a "bad hair day" was our special code for the way Mom and I felt when we were feeling down. It could be a day when you blew a big test, ruined your favorite shirt, or just felt blue and didn't know why. But mostly a "bad hair day" was a day that everything that could go wrong, did. I bet that girls like Leela or Camille never had a bad hair day in their lives—literally.

"Bleeeeeeep, bleeeeeeep!"

Yesss! Saved by the phone. I quickly asked to be excused, and raced to answer the line in the kitchen. It was Evonne.

"Girrrl, you missed it!" Evonne shouted.

"Missed what?"

"Mason said he liked you—right in front of Leela!"

"He what? Stop lying," I said, shaking my head in disbelief. Maybe things were looking up!

"I wouldn't play with you like that, Gab!" Evonne said.

My heart was racing and my stomach was flipping out all over the place.

"OK, Evonne, I need details," I said, trying to calm down.

"You know if you had a *cell* phone I could have called or texted you about this right after it happened."

"Right, like that'll ever happen. Just spill it already. And talk slow. I want ALL the details."

"Well, we were all hanging out after basketball and cheering practice and we started talking about you," Evonne said.

"About me?" I asked. "Why?"

"It just kind of happened. We were talking about one thing, then another, and it led to you," Evonne said. "OK, like we were all talking about how we needed new uniforms. Then we started talking about how the school could use better cafeteria food and a new this and a new that. You know how it is."

"Yeah," I said impatiently. I was well aware of the conditions at Lofton. It was a decent school, but it didn't have a lot of the perks I enjoyed at Thornton Prep.

"So I told them how great your school is," Evonne continued. "Then Leela started dogging you out saying you were a sell-out for going to a white school. Well, Mason started defending you. Then she said, 'Why are you so quick to take up for Gabby? Do you like her or something?' And that's when it happened."

"Uh-huh," I said, waiting to hear what I had always dreamed Mason would say about me.

"He didn't say a word," Evonne said.

OK. I was definitely missing something.

"And?"

"And what?" Evonne said.

"Evonne, he didn't say anything!" I shot back.

"Exactly!" she said. "If he didn't like you, he would have said 'No way!' or 'Girl, please!' but he just looked at her and smiled."

Her reasoning *kind of* made sense, but then again, his silence was hardly a confession of true love.

"There's more, girl," she said.

More? OK, now we get down to the good stuff.

"After the guys left, Leela got all upset and told everyone that you didn't know anything about boys and that you had never even been kissed," Evonne said.

"Really? I don't believe it," I said, fidgeting.

Well, actually I could, because it was true.

"I know. I told her I knew for a fact that you had kissed a boy. It happened when you went away for that church youth retreat last summer, right?"

"Oh, right," I said, remembering my less-than-honest description of my first kiss. I told everyone at Evonne's birthday sleepover that this guy Jason had led me off to a private spot a little ways from the trail on our afternoon hike. Then, surrounded by trees and sunlight, he gave me a slow, wonderful, *open-mouthed* kiss. But the real deal was that Jason and I were partners in an obstacle race. It was a half-mile course complete with tires, a rope climb, and monkey bars. We were the last team to get through it (my fault, not Jason's) and everyone was waiting because I was stuck on the monkey bars. I started out OK, but about halfway through I realized that I was winded and couldn't make it. Jason was doing his best to encourage me to finish, standing right by me to cheer me on, but it was no use. I lost my grip, ended up falling down on top of him, and somehow my mouth smacked dead on top of his. Everyone laughed as E. J. Gathers yelled, "Look, Gabby finally got her first kiss!" Actually, even though I didn't think so at the time, it was pretty funny—definitely YouTube-worthy.

Man, Mom really is right. I *do* have a bad habit of exaggerating. I hadn't been honest with Evonne at all. In my defense, I was caught off guard. Evonne's sleepover happened not too long after the retreat and everyone was telling their first kiss stories. Being the only one to say "Well, I'm actually still waiting for my first kiss" wasn't a very appealing option.

Evonne went on. "Well, she didn't believe it and said she and her crew would pay money to see you kiss *anyone*. She's so dramatic. Anyway, I said OK."

"What do you mean you said OK?"

"I told her that we accepted their bet."

At this rate, I was going to have a heart attack before I turned thirteen.

"Look, Evonne I—"

"I know, Gabby. This is *all* kinds of stupid, but I couldn't resist shutting Leela up. All you have to do is kiss Mason and—"

"Mason?" I cried. "Wait a minute, why Mason?"

"Well, actually Leela suggested that it be Mason. I think it's because she thinks you'll never kiss him. I uh…well… you do act kind of goofy around him."

"Goofy?" I said, annoyed at her observation. "Evonne, listen—"

Just then, Mom called, "Gabby! I need your help with the dishes!"

"Evonne, there is no way I'm doing that," I said.

"But all you have to do is kiss Mason and we each get twenty-five dollars!" Evonne said.

"Wrap it up *now*, Gabby!" Mom yelled.

"Look, Evonne, I've got to go," I said. "Talk to you tomorrow."

• • •

The next day, I needed to clear my head and think things through, so I went to the church. Reed Street was the only place Mom would let me travel to on my own. Dad had been there since the crack of dawn, as usual, handling church business. Sometimes I went, too, to help set up for the daily activities. There was always something going on. Choir practice, Bible study, youth ministry, church plays, you name it. Saturdays were always the busiest. The women of the church kicked off the day with their "Church Lady Workout," then there was soup kitchen and choir practice, followed by the usher board meeting and, every once in a while, a church play.

When I got there I headed straight to the basement, which had a kitchen and large hall for all sorts of receptions and events. The church's community aid committee was in the middle of soup kitchen—a crazy time. Everybody was running around, cooking, mixing, and getting tables ready. Mrs. Nixon rushed by carrying a stack of dinner rolls.

"Hey, Gabby," she said. "Are you helping out today? We sure could use you."

"Sure, Mrs. Nixon," I said and headed for the kitchen—the place where I felt most at home.

As always, the menu was simple: spaghetti, salad, rolls, lemonade, and chocolate chip cookies for dessert. Almost everything from the meal was made from a jar or box, but I was about to make it whole lot better with my special spices and ingredients. Mrs. Patterson was gathering plasticware and napkins as I entered the kitchen.

"Hey, Gabby," she said. "Are you about to work your magic on the sauce and cookies?"

"Yup, and I'll even add a little something to the lemonade," I said. "Everyone turn around."

All the people in the kitchen laughed and rolled their eyes. I was very secretive about my ingredients. Ma McGee said that it was the mark of a good cook. After locating my secret stash way back in one of the cupboards, I got to work. A little while later, everyone agreed that whatever I had done, the sauce was ten times better and the cookies were the best they'd ever tasted, so I started taking stuff outside to the serving area.

No matter how many times I helped out at the soup kitchen, I was always amazed by how many people came. And there were so many kids! I could never imagine living in the street, but—unfortunately—the street was home to every other kid in the room. My dad says that lots of folks blame the homeless for being lazy but don't realize that most people are only a paycheck away from living on the street. He also says it's our duty to help them. This issue always riles him up because as a minister, people always ask him why God lets bad things happen. Dad says that if everyone followed the example Jesus set and helped his fellow man, there wouldn't be a homeless person on Earth. He usually goes on and on about these things, which I guess is his job. And you can't really blame him. Every time I leave the soup kitchen, I feel something stirring up inside me, too.

In a matter of a few hours, we had gotten down to the last of the food. Unfortunately, there were still lots of people waiting at the door. This was happening a lot lately, and it was the worst. Dad usually handled the uneasy task of telling everyone, and today was no different.

"Pastor McGee," Mrs. Nixon called. "We've got to close up."

While everyone was eating, Dad had been walking around the tables talking to some of the people. He always used the meal as an opportunity to share the Word with those who were interested. As he headed to the door to give the bad news, I noticed someone familiar in the crowd. It was Derek Arrington! He looked a little different, though. Tired and, well, just different. I wanted to catch my dad to tell him who Derek was and see if there was something, *anything*, we could give him, but I was frozen in place. I didn't realize that things were that bad for his family. In fact, I'd be willing to bet nobody at school knew it was this bad. I didn't want Derek to feel worse than how he looked standing at that door being turned away, so I went back to the kitchen to help clean up. All of a sudden, my worries seemed very small.

It took a while, but we said goodbye to the last few stragglers. Dad went up to his office, and we finished cleaning up. As we were clearing the tables, a woman entered the side door of the basement.

"Good afternoon, can anyone help me?" she asked. "I'm looking for Reverend McGee."

She was very pretty, and dressed up as though she was here for Sunday service. She wore a beautiful cream pantsuit and black heels, her face was flawlessly made up, and her hair was slicked back in a neat bun.

"Sure. He's my dad," I said waving to her. "I can take you to him."

She thanked me and I pointed her to the stairwell. As we walked side by side up the stairs, I noticed that she seemed kind of stuck-up. She was very polite and didn't do or say anything wrong, but after being at Thornton Prep a couple of years, I could spot stuck-up a mile away. I also noticed that she looked a little familiar. When we got to Dad's office, I knocked on the door.

"Come in," he said.

"Hi, Dad, you have a visitor," I said as we entered his office.

"Hi, Reverend McGee, I'm Vivian LaRue," the woman said, extending her hand. "I wanted to talk to you about using your church for an event."

"Hello, Mrs. LaRue," my father said, rising from behind his desk. "I appreciate the interest, but unfortunately we only allow church-related activities to be held here."

Dad was very strict about that. He said that while other churches consented to having events like town meetings, dances, and even hair shows in their buildings, he discouraged hosting non-church events because he could never have complete control over what might happen.

"Well, Reverend, I completely understand, but I hope you'll hear me out," said Mrs. LaRue, helping herself to a seat on Dad's sofa.

"Of course," Dad said as he sat back down at his desk.

"You see my organization—The BluBelles—is having its first annual cake bake-off to raise money for charity," she said. "We were all set to have the competition at the Evanswood Country Club, but there was a terrible mishap at their facilities—some flooding or something like that—and it's going to take weeks to repair the damages."

"I'm sorry to hear that," Dad said.

"Well, our event is in two weeks," she continued. "We've searched and searched for another venue in Rodgers Park to no avail. We tried The Crystal Cove, The Silver Tea Room, and even The Brass Elephant. No one else can accommodate us on such short notice or at any other time for the rest of this year—everyone's booked."

Mrs. LaRue shifted on the sofa and her mood brightened.

"So I thought, why not 'go quaint.' I mean, this really isn't a typical BluBelle event, anyway. None of the BluBelles actually bake, but this year we're trying to pay homage to our founder and my grandmother, Elenora Blu Davis. She was a terrific baker. It was her passion, God rest her soul."

"I see," Dad said, still unconvinced.

"I've done my research," Mrs. LaRue said. "From what I've heard, your kitchen would be ideal for our bake-off."

She was right about that. The kitchen was huge, and earlier that year the church had received a donation of kitchen appliances and equipment from a local restaurant.

Dad still looked skeptical, though. "Believe me, Mrs. LaRue, I'm not trying to be unreasonable, but—"

"Did I mention that we've already raised close to twenty-five thousand dollars from contest entries, sponsorships, and donations that will all go directly to charity?" said Mrs. LaRue. "Unfortunately, we'll have to give it all back if we call off the event."

Mrs. LaRue wasn't new at this. She knew it would be hard for Dad to say no to that. As he mulled it over, his office door swung open.

"There you are, Mom! You're taking forever," said an obviously annoyed girl at the door. Make that an obviously annoyed Camille! I couldn't believe I hadn't put it together before. Mrs. LaRue was Camille's mom!

"It hasn't been that long, Camille," Mrs. LaRue said, looking slightly embarrassed. "And I did tell you that you were welcome to come in with me."

"Yeah, well, you said it wasn't going to take long to get them to say yes," Camille said as she walked past me and flopped down next to her mother on Dad's couch. "You *do* know I have a hair appointment in an hour."

Camille needed a hair appointment about as much as the LaRues needed more money. Her hair was perfect. Not surprisingly, she didn't acknowledge anybody's presence but instead turned her attention to texting on her phone.

"Reverend, this is my daughter Camille," Mrs. LaRue said hastily.

"Hi, Camille," Dad said.

She looked up, nodded, and then went back to texting.

Mortified yet determined, Mrs. LaRue went on. "So, can the BluBelles count on you? The money we raise is going to do so much good."

"OK, you got me. I can't say no to charity," he said, smiling. "But please understand that I have to insist on being kept in the loop on all the details and planning."

"Of course, Reverend McGee," she said, clearly relieved. "Thank you so much! You know, we're still accepting contestants if any of your congregants are interested. The entry fee is fifty dollars."

"Oh, I'm sure more than a few will be interested. In fact, I know of someone right here in this room," Dad said, nodding in my direction.

Normally I would jump at any chance to bake, but I had too many other things to worry about. I needed to figure out how to pay back Mrs. Henry, plus, the bake-off was on the same Saturday as the big game at Lofton.

"Aww, isn't that sweet," Mrs. LaRue said. "You can bake, dear?"

"Uh-huh," I said.

"Why would you make a cake when you could just *buy* one?" Camille asked. "Mom got me the cutest little birthday cake from Monroe's last year. It was in the shape of a Prada bag, and it only cost eight hundred dollars."

Mrs. LaRue looked like she wanted to slap Camille *and* bury her own head in her hands. Still, she pressed on. "Well, Camille, the contest rules stipulate that all entries *must* be made from scratch by the contestant," she said. "No box cakes. No canned frosting."

"No problem," I said.

"Gabby has been baking since she was eight," Dad said. "In fact, she just might win your contest."

"I don't know about that, Dad," I said.

"Why not? You have just as good a chance as anyone."

Dad seemed confident, but Mrs. LaRue didn't look like she believed him. She stood up to leave. "Well, Reverend, I'll be in touch. In the meantime, here's a personalized invitation with all the details. Thank you again."

"Finally!" Camille said as she rose. Walking past me again, she actually looked in my direction, narrowing her eyes like she might possibly recognize me. "Bye, Cake Girl," she said under her breath.

"Let's *go*, Camille," Mrs. LaRue said. And with that, they were gone and off to the hair appointment that couldn't wait.

"Do you know that girl?" Dad asked.

"Yeah. Well, no, not really," I said. "I don't *know* her, know her. She's just a girl from my school."

"Oh. Well, anyway, you should really look into this, Gabby," he said, reading the invitation. "The winner gets five hundred dollars!"

At that moment, I knew that God really does answer prayers! I couldn't believe it! Five hundred dollars! That prize would get me the money for Mrs. Henry's dryer and more than replenish my perm fund.

"Dad, do you really think I can do it?"

"Of course," he said.

"I know just what to bake," I said, grabbing the invite from Dad. "My famous six-layer, triple-chocolate cake!"

"It's always a winner with me," my dad agreed.

While it would be tempting to show off and build some flowery, ruffly, ten-tiered confection that looked like the wedding cake of the year, it would never taste as good as the six-layer chocolate masterpiece that no one I knew could resist.

"It says here that the entry fee must be sent to Mrs. LaRue," I said, reading the invite. "Dad, can you send the money in for me?"

"Sure. Just make sure to give it to me early next week."

"Huh?"

"The fifty dollars," Dad said. "Make sure to give it to me by Monday or Tuesday."

"Dad, I thought that—"

"You thought I was going to pop for this," he said.

"Well, yeah."

"No way," he said. "As I remember it, you've been pilfering away your allowance for quite a while. I think you can handle giving fifty dollars to charity."

He was right. As far as he knew, I had the contest entry fee and money to spare. And, if I hadn't gone behind my parent's back to go to the salon and allegedly break Mrs. Henry's dryer, I would have. But now I couldn't pay the fee and there was no way I could tell him why. Man! Just when I thought I had a way out of this mess. But then I realized, I actually did.

Six

Sunday was a blur. I spent most of the morning church service worrying about how I would get up the nerve to do what had to be done. And Sunday night, I dreamed that I was trapped inside a cake with loads of layers, and every time I thought I had gotten out of it, another layer fell on top of me. It was one of those dreams where you know that you're dreaming and try really hard to wake up but can't. Ma McGee calls it "having a witch on your back." Anyway, when I finally woke up Monday morning I was covered by all of my pillows, drenched in sweat, and exhausted from trying to get out of that cake.

"Gabby, it's time to get up!" Mom called.

I knew exactly what I had to do, but it wouldn't be easy. Luckily, Mom was running late again that day, so I had time to meet Evonne at the bus stop.

"Hey . . . your hair!" she said. "You didn't get—"

"Yeah, I know. My hair is jacked up," I said. And was it ever. Mom had braided it wet Sunday night thinking that I'd wake up, we'd remove the braids, and I'd have a head full of waves and curls. Unfortunately, my hair is like a sponge. It was still wet when I woke up and once all of the braids were out, it was a damp, nappy mess. Mom threw a headband over it to help rein it in, but it still looked crazy. However, for once, I had more pressing matters to deal with.

"Hey, do you have fifty bucks you could loan me?" I asked Evonne already knowing the answer.

"Girl, please," she said. "You know I spend money as fast as I get it. My mom cut me off last week. Why do you think I was so excited about Leela's bet?"

"I didn't know, but it was worth a shot. OK, then, let's do it."

"Do what?"

I rolled my eyes. "Look, if you think Leela would still take us up on that bet, I'm willing to kiss Mason."

Evonne's eyes got big. "Really? Oh, great, girl. This will be the easiest twenty-five dollars I've ever made. Actually, it will be the only twenty-five bucks I've ever made."

"Yeah, about that," I said. "I'm going to need the whole fifty dollars."

"Why?"

Then, like the air rushing out of a balloon that's burst, everything came out—the dryer incident... the bake-off... everything.

"Man, you really got yourself in deep," Evonne said, shaking her head. "All right, the fifty dollars is yours. It will be worth it just to see Leela's face. Plus, we've got to win this bet now. If your mom finds out about Mrs. Henry's dumb dryer, that means no *Jill Jones* for you *or* me."

I gave Evonne a huge hug, but I still didn't feel much better. Out of the corner of my eye I spied Leela rounding the corner with her girls.

"Hey, Evonne! Hey, Gabby," Leela said when they reached the stop.

"Hey, Leela," Evonne said. "Well, it looks like you're going to owe us fifty dollars soon."

"What?" she said in disbelief.

"Gabby's going to kiss Mason and win your little bet," Evonne bragged.

"Yeah, right," said Leela, flipping her hair and turning to face me. "You do know that you have to give him a *real* kiss, don't you?"

"Yeah, I know," I mumbled.

"That means a French kiss," she teased. "Do you even know what that is, Nappy—oh, sorry, I mean, Gabby?"

Her girls started howling. They didn't even try to contain themselves. My face was hot like I was wearing a thousand sweaters—but for once no cotton balls! Even better, I seemed know exactly what to say.

"Yeah, I know what it is," I said with more confidence than I'd ever had in my life. "And pretty soon Mason will know just how well I know. So have my money ready, all right?"

And with that, I turned and headed to the car, wondering how I'd ever been able to say what I just said. I could hear her girls laughing and clowning her, and I was positive that Evonne's jaw was on the ground.

"Dang, Leela," Kameira said, laughing. "She sure told you!"

"Shut up," Leela said.

I got her good, and it felt great. But I was scared out of my mind.

• • •

On Tuesday, Evonne went to Mason and told him that I liked him. She said he smiled and asked if he could have my number. When she told him that I actually wanted to meet up with him, she said he smiled real hard, nodded, and said, "I get it. Her pops or her moms is always around. That's why I never really stepped to her. Plus, her dad's a minister."

"Yeah, right," Evonne agreed. "Well, anyway, she wants to meet up with you at the pre-victory dance."

"I thought she couldn't go to dances," he said, surprised.

"Don't worry," Evonne assured him. "She'll be there."

She explained that I couldn't stay very long but maybe we could share a dance. He thought it was kind of strange, but he agreed. Evonne and I planned to tell my folks that I would be staying over her house on the night of the dance. We would tell Evonne's mom that my folks had finally agreed to let me go to a Lofton party with her. This part would be tricky. Everyone in town seemed to know that my parents didn't let me do anything. But Evonne seemed to think she could handle her mom. Anyway, at the dance, I would get Mason to go outside with me in the hall where there would be plenty of kids milling around as witnesses— and then I'd kiss him. It sounded simple, but I had no idea how I was going to pull it off. I'd never kissed anyone, and now I had to have my very *first* kiss . . . *with Mason* . . . in front of *everyone*. I'd imagined this moment a thousand times in my head, but not this way. It was the most embarrassing thing that I could ever imagine doing, but it had to be done. All because I couldn't wait to have straight hair. But if you asked Evonne, it was all good. In fact, it was going to be the thing that changed my life. Which was funny, because that was the same exact thing she'd told me when *she* made the hair appointment in the first place. Anyway, according to her I just needed to relax. And isn't this what I wanted all along? But his tongue—*our* tongues—actually . . . touching? I'd only seen those kinds of kisses on TV. And I'd never even been that close to a boy before. How would I hold my head? Where would I put my hands? I had no clue, but I also had no choice. I had to repay Mrs. Henry, and this was the only way I had of getting the money. Well, it was actually the *start* of the only way I had of getting it. After I won the bet, I *still* had to bake the best cake for the BluBelles' First Annual Cake Bake-Off. If everything worked out, I'd avoid Mom's wrath *and* make sure that Evonne and I would still get to see Jasmine Jeffers, aka *Jill Jones: Girl Detective* in person. It was a hot mess. How did things go so wrong, so fast? It's funny how everything can be good and right in your world one day and then the next day you're facing the embarrassment of your life, the death of a dream, and, possibly, the butt whippin' of your life.

• • •

Wednesday brought even bigger worries. I had a big algebra test that I hadn't even cracked a book for. In fact, I hadn't been giving much attention to any of my classes with everything that was going on. On the way to the test, I had my head in my book, studying algebra for all it was worth. I wasn't paying attention and ran right smack into Camille, of all people, knocking her down. And even though it was just Camille, I felt like a jerk for not looking where I was going, so I immediately began apologizing.

"Sorry, I was just—"

"Was just what?" she asked, brushing herself off as Taylor Bennett—one of her snob mobsters—helped her to her feet. "Being clumsy?"

"Look, I'm sorry," I said. "I have a big test and I wasn't paying attention."

"Well, maybe if you had studied, this wouldn't have happened," she said. "You're lucky I'm only wearing this stupid uniform and not a real outfit."

Was she for real? I noticed she had her phone in hand, but I'm sure that the possibility that her constant texting had contributed to our collision never crossed her mind.

"Hey," she said, really looking at me for the first time. "You're Cake Girl!"

"Huh?"

"Cake Girl," she repeated. "I saw you last weekend. My mom's group is having their stupid baking contest at your church."

"Baking contest?" asked Taylor.

"Yeah, it's something my mom's silly group is doing for charity, and I guess Cake Girl here is going to be a contestant. I swear my mom is in some old school time warp. They call themselves the BluBelles. My great grandmother started it years ago, so my mom had to join. It's so lame."

"So I guess you're a future BluBelle," said Taylor, giggling. "Better get 'Cake Girl' here to teach you how to turn on an oven."

That sent the others rolling, and even I cracked a smile even though I was somewhat part of the joke. Camille, however, was not amused and shot Taylor a nasty look that stopped the laughs right away. Man, she had those girls in check!

"There's no way I'm becoming a BluBelle," said Camille. "Even though Cake Girl *should* be honored that they are having the contest at her church. They're lame, but they do have a lot of power."

"Then why are they having it at her church?" asked Taylor.

"If you *must* know, some people in Rodgers Park are a little mad about one of Daddy's business ventures. But Daddy says not to worry. Everything will be back to normal once things with his friend are cleared up. Until then, Mom says we may have to suffer a few inconveniences. Like Mom not having access to Evanswood or The Crystal Cove and me not getting a private appointment with André at Salon One. Would you believe I had to get my hair done by Melanie and I was almost late for *that* appointment waiting for Mother?"

So, the BluBelles weren't the victims of mysterious mishaps or bad timing. It was the LaRues! Right now their name was mud. Well good. I know it wasn't nice, but I was glad to know that they hadn't escaped totally clean from their financial fiasco. After hearing that, I was ready to go. If "Cake Girl" was going have any chance at passing her algebra test, she had to at least show up for it. Plus, they had forgotten I was standing there and had moved on to other things.

"So what's up with Derek? Are you guys really done?" Taylor asked as I turned to walk away.

"Of course," Camille said, laughing. "His family has nothing."

Unbelievable. The girl just didn't care. Maybe this is what Dad meant when he said that the love of money was the root of all evil. Suddenly, I felt a chill down my spine, and it had nothing to do with Camille.

"Ladies, the class bell will be ringing soon," said Headmaster Brookfield, appearing out of nowhere behind us. "I'm sure you'll want to start moving—with haste!"

Where did he come from? We all scattered like bugs— quiet, focused bugs—to our classes. Brooksie was one creepy dude.

Seven

*A*ll week I was so nervous about the dance that I didn't even meet Evonne at the bus stop for our morning download. I was afraid that I'd see Mason and call the whole thing off. What's worse, I waited until the very last minute to tell my folks that I'd be sleeping over at Evonne's. It was like, until I asked their permission, it wasn't real. I could pretend everything was normal and that I wasn't about to lie about going to the dance or have a real kiss with someone I couldn't even work up the nerve to talk to.

But now it was Friday evening, two hours before the dance, and I was in the kitchen making Quiche Lorraine and roasted potatoes while trying to figure out how to ask Mom about sleeping over at Evonne's without making her suspicious. She had just gotten home from work and walked in looking exhausted.

"Hey, Gabby," Mom said, kissing me on the cheek and rubbing her head. "Where's Ma McGee?"

"Upstairs," I said. "You OK?"

"Yeah, just a little headache. Is that dinner I smell?" she asked, taking in the aroma coming from the oven.

"Yup. Quiche," I said.

"Oh, Gab, that's great," she said, plopping her laptop case on the counter. "I'm so happy you didn't take after me in the cooking department."

"Yeah, so is everyone else, especially Dad," I laughed. "I actually thought that after Ma McGee left, you guys could enjoy this dinner alone together...while I stayed over Evonne's tonight."

"Oh, really," she said with a smirk. "You've got everything worked out, huh? Well, as nice of a gesture as this is, I suspect that this has a lot more to do with you trying to do something you and Evonne shouldn't be doing than with giving your dad and I some alone time."

"Huh?" I said, suddenly worried. *Did she know? How could she?*

"I know you watch music videos at Evonne's," she said. "You know I don't like you watching those, *or* springing sleepovers on me at the last minute."

"Well, um . . ." I stammered.

"It's OK, Gabby," she said, smiling. "I get it. I was I kid once too. Anyway, it's all right if you stay over."

Yessss! This was going to work out. I'd make a brief appearance at the dance, kiss Mason, and leave.

"Oh, one thing," Mom said, interrupting my thoughts. "I'll be enjoying my quiche alone tonight. Your dad has to give some speech or something."

"Oh, shoot," I said. "Where?"

"You know . . . I don't even remember," Mom said. "It was a last-minute thing he mentioned to me today. To tell the truth, I was so busy with this case I'm working on that I wasn't really paying attention. Don't tell him that, though."

"Sure, Mom," I said. "Well, anyway, maybe he'll be home early enough for you guys to enjoy dessert together."

"Dessert?"

"Yeah, I made my triple-fudge brownies."

"Gabby, you are hands down the world's greatest daughter," Mom said, heading upstairs to change.

World's greatest daughter or world's greatest liar?

• • •

If I did say so myself, I looked great. I couldn't believe it, but my hair was straight, silky smooth, and past my shoulders! Plus, I had a real outfit on, not something my mom had picked out for me to wear. I kind of felt like Cinderella. My fairy godmother, Evonne, had come with her mom to pick me up before the dance so that I could raid her closet to find the perfect outfit. Once I settled on a purple turtleneck, denim mini, and matching tights, Evonne went about the business of convincing me to take out my cornrows.

"Look, you want to look your best, right?" she asked as we looked at my outfit in her closet mirror.

"Yeah, but—"

"But nothing," she said. "Your cornrows look pretty good, but—no offense—they're just . . . not . . . hot."

I inspected myself even more closely in her mirror. I had gotten Ma McGee to do my hair while she was at our house. I could tell Mom was hurt, but I was not going to look like a crazy person at my first dance—especially since I planned on seeing and *kissing* Mason. But Evonne was right. The cornrows were cute, but not hot.

"Once we get these braids out, I'll press and curl it myself," Evonne said, easing me down in the chair in front of her vanity.

Evonne's hair always looked really good, so I was confident that she could work her magic on mine, too. And she did. After about an hour, I hardly recognized myself. It was exactly what I'd wanted all of these years!

"Girl, you look good! You'll definitely have Mason's attention tonight," Evonne said as she coiled the power cord around her curling iron. "And why exactly have you waited so long to do this?"

"Mom has a thing about using heat on my hair, too," I said rolling my eyes. "And remember, I've been a fashion *don't* without even knowing it for twelve years. Plus, I honestly didn't think it would work. My hair is pretty tough."

"Girl, please. My cousin Jordyn flat irons her hair every day, and her hair is a lot nappier than yours. You should be in good shape tonight, too. There's not a cloud in the sky. But hey, are you sure you want to wear that turtleneck?"

"Yeah, why not? It's perfect," I said, admiring myself in the mirror. "Besides, it's freezing tonight."

"Yeah, but it can get hot up in there sometimes. Especially when the heat's not working right," she warned. "Just don't dance too hard, or you'll melt."

"Don't worry, I won't," I said, flipping my hair from side to side. "Besides, I'm not really going there to dance. Right?"

As Evonne's mother drove us to the dance, she went on and on about her days at Lofton and how different things were from today.

"First of all, we never had *pre*-victory parties," Mrs. Edwards said. "I mean, who's ever even heard of a pre-victory party? I wouldn't have believed the school would have allowed it except I know Principal Jones. She's a real trip."

We giggled in the back of her SUV.

"Well, you're right on that one, Mom," Evonne agreed. "But actually, this game is pretty much in the bag already. Lofton is going to cream Thornton, and then it's off to the state tournament. No offense, Gab."

"None taken," I said, playing with the hair on my shoulders. "Believe me, I know Thornton doesn't have a prayer."

"Speaking of prayers," Mrs. Edwards said, "I guess you'll be happy to see your dad at the dance tonight."

Evonne and I looked at each other.

"Huh?" I said, confused.

I didn't think I heard her right. *My* dad? *My* dad at the *dance? Tonight?*

"Yeah, you know, it's part of the festivities," she said. "To inspire the team, they're bringing back some of the old players from the team that won Lofton's only state championship."

"Oh," I said, sinking into my seat. No wonder she thought it was OK for me to go to the dance. She thought Dad would be there with me!

"Yeah, I ran into Mason's mom, Kim, at Shear Wonders today, and she was going on and on about it," she continued. "You guys know I went to Lofton Middle with your dad—and Mason's parents, too, Gabby. Well, Kim does just as much bragging on Mike as she did back then—maybe even more. She told me that the best players from the old championship team were invited to speak, and they asked that your dad say a prayer."

There was no way I could let Dad see me at the dance! What was I going to do?

"Yeah, Kim was in all her glory today," Mrs. Edwards said. "The shop was packed and she talked from the time she walked through the door until she left. From the Wilkes' divorce to the Arrington's problems, I think I heard about everything going on in Lofton and the surrounding counties. You know, I don't even think Kim needed to get her hair done. She just couldn't wait to tell everybody's business. By the way, you didn't tell me how bad off the Arringtons were, Evonne."

"I don't know anything about that Mom," Evonne said, looking confused at me. "Do you, Gabby?"

Dang! With everything going on with Mason and the contest, I'd forgotten about Derek.

"Well, yeah, kind of. Hannah told me they were having money problems and Derek had to quit Thornton," I said, leaving out the part about seeing Derek at the soup kitchen.

"Yeah, well, it's worse than Derek having to leave private school," Mrs. Edwards said. "They lost everything, and now they're homeless."

"Homeless?" Evonne said, shocked.

"Yeah, Derek's dad got hooked up into some crazy money scheme with some rich guy—Miles LaRue, I think— and lost all their money. Kim said Derek's mom begged his dad not to invest everything, but he told her that if they wanted to be really rich like the LaRues, they had to think rich and be aggressive. I guess this Miles LaRue was feeding him a lot of nonsense about how his lotto winnings wouldn't last that long these days, and if he wanted to guarantee financial security for generations to come, he would have to quadruple that—at least. I guess he even guaranteed that it was a sure thing and that he could double his money in a few months."

Evonne shook her head in disbelief. And, like her, I still didn't get it. If I had that kind of dough, I wouldn't risk it. Of course my financial know-how comes from a Baptist preacher who believes money should be saved, not spent. Dad would never risk twenty dollars, let alone twenty million.

Evonne's mom went on. "I feel sorry for the family, but that's what Derek's dad gets for trying to keep up with the Joneses. Or, in this case, the LaRues. The man won over twenty million dollars! You'd think he'd be grateful for that. Shoot, I'd be grateful for just one million."

"Do you think they'll be all right, Mom?" Evonne asked, reading my mind.

"I don't know, Vonnie. Times are tough these days. And according to Kim, Mr. Arrington refuses to live with relatives. He's too embarrassed. He's trying to get back on at the Clemmons plant, but it doesn't look good," Mrs. Edwards said as she wheeled up to the gym entrance. "Well, here we are."

We sat stuck in our seats.

"What's up?" Mrs. Edwards said, looking at us through her rearview mirror. "Are you guys going in or what?"

There was no way I could go in, but there was also no way I could explain to Mrs. Edwards how I forgot to mention that I wasn't even allowed to go to the dance in the first place. We had to go and figure something else out along the way.

"Yeah, we're going," I said as I looked at Evonne and climbed out of my seat.

Before we even got inside, we heard the music blasting from the gym—but it looked like the party was in the halls. Kids were everywhere talking, laughing, and hanging out against lockers. One of the teachers was walking around fussing.

"I don't get it," she said, trying to round everyone up to go back inside the gym. "The music and refreshments are all in the gym, and you're all jammed out here as hot as it is."

Evonne warned me that at Lofton parties, cool kids hung out in the halls when they weren't dancing, while the nerds walked around in the gym. I would have been more at home inside the gym, but tonight I was on a mission. If I could avoid Dad and spot Mason, I could plant one on him and hide out in the girl's bathroom until Evonne's mom came for us. We walked up and down the halls, but there was no sign of him.

"Are you sure he's coming?" I asked Evonne as my eyes searched the hallway for Mason *and* my dad.

"Of course he's coming," she said. "He's on the team, right? He's probably just late."

"Yeah, right," I said. "Man, it's hot. Are you hot, or is it just me?"

"I told you," Evonne said. "It's the furnace. Sometimes, it gets too hot no matter what they do. Just one of many things that need fixing around here."

Evonne's purple turtleneck looked great on me, but I was starting to think that she was right. It might not have been the best choice for tonight. Evonne reassured me.

"You may feel hot, but you look hot, too," she said. "All the guys are staring at you. Haven't you noticed?"

She was right. I'd never had guys look at me this way before. Part of me couldn't believe it was so simple. All I had to do was change my hair and I could get the kind of attention I wanted. But it was also kind of weird. I was the same person I was before Evonne flat ironed my hair. Was this *all* guys wanted?

"Hey, why didn't you tell me about Derek?" Evonne asked.

"Believe it or not, with everything going on it kind of slipped my mind," I said. "Besides, I wasn't sure he'd want everyone to know."

"Yeah, but I'm your best friend."

"You're right. In that case, you should probably know that Camille broke up with him."

"What?"

"I know. I keep telling Hannah what a phony she is."

"I thought Hannah had figured that out on her own."

"Yeah, I thought so, too."

"Well, what can we do for Derek?" Evonne said.

"I'm not sure," I said. "My dad says that all the local shelters are full."

We thought about it as we walked. There was no quick fix for this.

"Hannah's working on trying to get Thornton to lend a hand," I offered.

"Really?"

"Uh-huh. She's trying to raise money and get the school to provide Derek with a full scholarship for the year."

Evonne rolled her eyes. "Why is she trying to do that?"

I looked at her, puzzled.

"I mean, I think they have bigger concerns than him getting back into Thornton," she said.

"You're right," I said. "But I don't think Hannah knows they're homeless. And from what it sounds like, Derek's dad wouldn't allow him to take a scholarship anyway."

"But he can come back here to Lofton where he's wanted," she said. "Thornton has a lot, but it doesn't have a lock on a good education. "You don't need a state-of-the-art science lab to learn that H_2O is the symbol for water or a special theatre to study Shakespeare."

I nodded. Everyone thinks Thornton's so hot. Evonne is a straight-A student and is as smart as anyone I know at Lofton *or* Thornton. But figuring out Derek's situation was going to have to wait, because we had just spied Mason, his dad, and *my* dad walking into the school together. Evonne grabbed my arm and dragged me into the girl's locker room.

"Whew! That was close! Now what?" I said, breathing heavily.

"I'll go tell Mason to meet you in here," Evonne said. "Kiss him, get rid of him, and wait in here until I come get you."

"You make it sound so easy," I said. "Besides, that's not gonna work. Leela wants proof. And unless you can convince them to move the dance into the locker room, no one's gonna know about it."

"I know," she said waving her phone in my face. "After Mason comes in, I'll duck in here and snap a pic of you guys. As long as I get him in here, everything will work out just fine."

"OK, genius," I said nervously. "Just make sure I don't end up on Facebook or something."

"Why not?" she teased. "You'd finally get some much-needed street cred. Actually, you're getting the sweet end of this deal. I'd kiss Mason for fifty dollars any day."

After Evonne left, I waited in the dark with the lockers, gym equipment, and my thoughts. The truth was, I had given no thought as to how I'd actually bring myself to kiss Mason. Then I started to think that maybe I had been thinking about this all wrong. I mean, I had been waiting on my first kiss for years and had imagined it in my head a hundred times. Sometimes it was with a singer or TV star, but these days it was mostly with Mason. And I always had thick, long, straight hair that he ran his fingers through and said was beautiful. Then he'd run of both his hands along the side of my face, pull me close and give me the greatest kiss ever. Maybe my dream was all coming true. I mean, I finally had the hair. But I never imagined it would be this hot! The locker room was even warmer than the hall, and I was starting to sweat. Evonne needed to hurry up and get Mason in here. Suddenly—*swish!* I heard the sound of the locker room door swing open. This was it. Well, at least it would be dark until Evonne came in. Mason wouldn't be able to see how nervous I was.

I saw a shadowy figure that I couldn't quite make out, but seeing that it was about my height, it definitely was *not* Mason. The light came on suddenly, and after I blinked a few times, I saw Leela in front of me.

"Waiting for someone?" she asked.

My human mute button came on again. I couldn't help it. Girls like Leela intimidated me. I guess the boldness I felt the last time I saw her had been temporary. Unfortunately, my silence didn't stop her from continuing her investigation.

"What are you doing here, anyway? You don't go to Lofton, and everyone knows your parents won't let you go to dances."

"What are you trying to pull, Leela?" said a voice from behind.

Evonne to the rescue!

Leela spun around. "What are you talking about?" As if she didn't know.

"You know what I mean," Evonne said. "Just now, out in the hall. I told Mason to meet Gabby in here, and he was on his way until you stopped him."

"I just told him that his father needed him in the gym," she said. "How was I supposed to know where he was going?"

"Mm-hmm," Evonne said, rolling her eyes.

"I can't help it if his dad needed him or if Afro Lady here can't kiss out in the open like a normal person," Leela said.

Afro Lady? What the heck was she talking about?

"Besides, she looks scared," she continued. "Let's just call this off, and you guys can give me my fifty dollars."

As I stood there feeling hotter and sweatier with every second, it sounded like a great idea to me. As much as I needed the money, I *was* scared to kiss Mason. For once, Leela and I were in agreement. Evonne, however, had other ideas.

"Oh, please, Leela," Evonne said. "The bet is still on. As a matter of fact, I can guarantee we're going to win. Unless you try to sabotage us again, that is."

With that, Evonne grabbed me and headed for the door.

"Time to go," she said under her breath. "Your dad is about to give his speech in the gym, I just called my mom to tell her I wasn't feeling well, and your hair just turned into a pumpkin, Cinderella."

As we made our exit, I caught a glimpse of myself in a wall of mirrors. The heat had turned my hair from Cinderella's to circus clown's.

Eight

The strawberry-banana-orange twister I got from Smoothie Operator was now all over my shirt. Blindsided by a stressed out mom with a stroller, my favorite orange-red concoction was a less-than-artistic splotch on my favorite white skinny-fit polo. It was bad enough that I was stuck at the Avalon Mall with my parents on a Saturday night. Now I had to suffer through it looking like a hot mess, too.

"I'm covered in smoothie, Mom!" I pleaded as we left the food court. "We've got to go."

"You are not *covered* in smoothie," Mom said. "It's just a little spill. Besides, we're almost done, and I really need to use this coupon. It expires tomorrow."

Little spill? And she says *I* exaggerate. I had tried to convince my folks to go to the less popular Golden Galleria like we usually do. But Mom had a 30-percent-off coupon to use on a blouse that was already 40-percent-off at Macy's. Of course the only Macy's in the area happens to be at Avalon Mall—*the* kid hangout. As we walked, I tried to keep my head down and stay on the lookout at the same time. I could tell that Dad was a little tense, too. I think he was starting to regret the day Vivian LaRue had set foot in his church. He had asked that she keep him in the loop on all the bake-off activities, and she'd kept to her word. In fact, Mrs. LaRue insisted that Dad attend all of the BluBelle Bake-Off meetings, which were held every day. Incredibly, this little cake contest was beginning to be a lot bigger than anyone could have imagined. Within a week's time, it turned into an all-day event that included a luncheon and formal program with speakers and activities. While Mrs. LaRue wasn't exactly high on people's list these days, the rest of the BluBelles still had friends in high places and used their influence to get the mayor to attend. They also convinced one of the local television stations to cover the event. This sent the Reed Street staff into overdrive cleaning and sprucing up the church. Mrs. LaRue was also using a lot of church resources and staff to accommodate her requests. Mrs. Nixon, the church secretary, was fielding calls from the mayor's office, caterers, and florists—plus, the usher board would be at her full disposal during the event.

"All this for a few cakes?" my mom asked as we entered Macy's.

"You don't understand, Eva," Dad said. "This is a full-day program with the choir singing, and the mayor is giving a big speech. I know it sounds crazy, but they've raised a lot of money for charity—over one hundred thousand dollars!"

"What? I thought it was twenty-five thousand dollars," Mom said.

"It was, but when they got the mayor on board, it caused a chain reaction," he said.

"Just this week, they got the word out, started selling tickets, and got a boatload of donations from local businesses. This little bake-off is now officially a big deal."

"I don't get it," she said, shaking her head.

"I know. The BluBelles must have something on the mayor," Dad joked.

"Well, anyway, it's for a good cause," Mom said. "Where is the money going?"

"Now *that* I don't know," Dad said. "It's supposed to be a big surprise to be revealed at the bake-off."

"I thought you were supposed to be in on everything," Mom said.

"I was," Dad said. "And not knowing makes me a little nervous. But her keeping the charity a secret is about right for Vivian. She's pretty dramatic."

I was getting nervous about the bake-off, too. I hadn't officially entered yet, but Mrs. LaRue told me that she would make an exception and accept my money on the day of the contest next Saturday. Still, I was cutting it close. Last night was a disaster, and I still hadn't figured out what to do about the bet. Evonne still wanted to go through with it. She was dying to show up Leela *and* see *Jill Jones*. But I wasn't so sure anymore. What if Leela was right and I chickened out? Then I would be humiliated and more in debt than I already was. All of my friends were as broke as I was... except . . . oh, man, Hannah! I couldn't believe I had forgotten. Sure, we were just getting to know each other, but I'm sure she wouldn't mind—and this was no time to be proud. Shoot, one hundred thirteen dollars is probably chump change to her. It would take me some time to pay Hannah back, but hey, this was the most hassle-free, responsible solution. Plus, there was no way for me to get into any more trouble. I was starting to feel more relaxed already. Then I felt a tap on my shoulder. I turned around to see Mason looking down at me. Like every other normal kid, he was hanging out at the mall with his friends on a Saturday night. DaShawn and Tommy hung behind him, smirking and looking at my messed-up shirt.

"Hey, what's up?" he asked.

Man, he looked good. He had on a navy Adidas warm-up suit and sneakers, and I noticed his fresh hair cut. A lot of guys wore cornrows, locs, or big Afros, but he kept his hair cut real close which I loved. He smelled great, too. Clean and fresh. *Go away, sweaters! Get lost, cotton balls! You can do this,* I told myself. *You can talk to him.*

"Hey, guys," I said.

"Hey, what happened?" Mason asked.

"Oh, this?" I said, pointing to my shirt. "Some lady ran into me and—"

"Not your shirt—I mean, what happened last night?"

Uh, my dad my showed up and I had to leave because I can't go, like, anywhere?

I couldn't say that, but I couldn't think of anything else. Luckily, I didn't have to.

"Hi, boys," Dad said, back just in time to save me from myself. Mom and Dad seemed to appear as suddenly as Mason and his friends had.

"Oh, hi Reverend McGee," Mason said.

"What *did* happen last night, Gabby?" Mom asked.

Once again, I had no answer. This time, Mason did.

"Oh... well... I just thought that since Reverend McGee was at the dance Friday night...Gabby would be there, too."

"Actually, I did think about letting Gabby go," Dad said.

I cringed. *Letting Gabby go.* Did he have to say it like that?

"But she already had plans with Evonne," he continued.

"Yeah, well, she missed an excellent prayer, sir," he said. "Very inspirational."

Mom rolled her eyes. I guess he *was* laying it on a little thick. It was time to go.

"Yeah, well, I guess we'd better get going," I said.

"Yeah . . . your shirt," Mason said trying to help.

"We do need to get going, Robert," Mom said to Dad. "I've got so much work to do it's not even funny."

"OK, boys. We'll see you later," Dad said. "Keep practicing. We're all pulling for you to make it to the state championship this year."

"That trophy is already ours, Reverend McGee. See you, Gabby," he said, winking at me.

He winked! Mom looked annoyed, but I was soaring and suddenly a teensy bit sorry that I'd probably be getting the money I needed from Hannah. I guess I could *still* go through with the bet. But who was I kidding? All this sneaking around was making me crazy. Maybe one day I'd have a chance with Mason, but for now I just planned to get the money I needed from Hannah so I could stop the madness.

• • •

Of course, like everything else, getting the money from Hannah wasn't as easy as I thought it would be. First off, she was out sick Monday and Tuesday, and she was asleep every time I tried calling her. On Wednesday, she was so busy catching up with her schoolwork and clubs, I barely saw her in the halls. Finally, on Thursday I caught up with her in gym class. Running up and down the field trying to kick a soccer ball wasn't the ideal way to ask for a loan, but it would have to do.

"Hey, Hannah, how are you feeling?" I asked trying to make conversation. I was anxious, but I couldn't just come right out and ask her like I would if it were Evonne. My friendship with Hannah was still new, and I didn't want to offend her.

"Better, but gym's hard today," she said. "I'm winded already."

"Me, too, and I wasn't even sick," I said.

Tired or not, we had to keep moving. Our gym teacher Miss Burns was big on class participation and not so big on "slackers."

"Look alive, girls!" she shouted as we ran past her. We tried our best as we huffed and puffed our way down the field.

"How's everything going with the fundraising for Derek?"

"You know, you'd think that in a place like Rodgers Park we would have had the money by now."

"The bake sale isn't going so well, huh?" I asked.

"No, and I don't think the car wash will, either."

"Let me guess, the Snob Mob took over, huh?"

Hannah rolled her eyes. She explained that Camille had convinced a bunch of her friends not to participate. She told them that if you wanted to go Thornton you should have to pay for it. Otherwise, *anybody* could go, and her mom didn't pay thousands of dollars for her to go to school with just anybody.

"She said that it's bad enough the school gives out partial scholarships," Hannah said. "And how Thornton's reputation would go downhill if they started giving *everyone* free rides."

I fumed. Who did she think she was? Kids like her made me remember why I hated going to Thornton Prep.

"See, this is just why I have no 'school spirit' as you like to say. All the rich kids here think they own the place and that kids like me should be falling over all them, thanking them for the privilege to come to here."

"Well, I'm going to try to talk to Camille to see if she'll come around," Hannah said. "Unfortunately, most of Thornton seems to follow her lead on things."

"Yeah, and you should know that better than anyone else," I said. "Why even talk to her? You know it's not going to do any good. Anyway, I thought you guys weren't even friends anymore."

"We're not. I mean, not really. Camille's mom is pretty good friends with my mom, so I can't completely avoid her. Besides, she's not so bad."

I couldn't believe it. She was defending her—again. Camille was just a richer version of Leela in my book. Actually, she was worse.

"I don't think Derek would agree," I said.

"Look, I know she's wrong about this whole scholarship thing, but—"

"But what? Camille is the biggest snob at Thornton. But I guess you don't care. Maybe you guys are more alike than I thought."

"That's crazy, and you know it," she said.

"Look, you can just end your little experiment with being a 'regular' girl. It's obviously not working, so just run back to Camille. I'm sure she'd be willing to take you back into the mob."

I regretted that as soon as I said it. Actually, I couldn't believe I said it. I guess Hannah couldn't believe it either, because she stopped and just stood there with her mouth hanging open as the other girls in class ran past her.

Tweeet!

Ms. Burns' whistle ended gym class, and Hannah ran off before I could say anything else. Not that I could have spoken then. It's really hard to talk with your foot stuck in your mouth.

Nine

This whole situation was getting out of hand. I still didn't have a guaranteed way to get the money I needed. And now I'd probably lost Hannah as a friend. I had to try to reason with Mrs. Henry again. I just needed more time. If I could convince her to let me pay her back in installments, this could all be over. Jill Jones never shied away from a sticky situation, so I decided it was time for me to meet this head on. This time I took Evonne with me. I'd convinced her to meet me at my house after school and Ma McGee to make us a snack while we "took a walk."

"And why, exactly, are we headed to Shear Wonders?" Evonne asked as we walked.

"I told you," I said, "I need to convince Mrs. Henry to let me off the hook."

"I don't think that's going to happen. You know how she is."

"Well, I've got to try, and maybe you can help this time."

"I don't know. Mrs. Henry kind of scares me."

"Me, too. Why do you think I brought you? Besides, don't you want to see *Jill Jones?*"

"Yeah, OK. I guess it's worth a try."

When we got to the shop, it was kind of dead. There was only one customer who was with another stylist, which was good because I needed Mrs. Henry's full attention. We walked right past Miss Fingernails at the front desk to Mrs. Henry's hairdresser station.

"Hi, Mrs. Henry, I wanted to talk to you about your dryer," I said, trying my best to sound friendly and sincere.

"You mean my *new* dryer," she said. "Have you got my money?"

"Uh, well, not exactly I—"

"Well, good" she said.

"Huh?" I said. Could she have changed her mind? Did Mrs. Henry have a heart after all?

"Well, it'll save you from havin' to get more money later," she said.

"I don't understand," I said.

"Yeah, what do you mean?" Evonne piped in.

Mrs. Henry turned to Evonne, annoyed. "Who are you, lil' girl?"

"I'm just her friend," Evonne said, clearly shaken.

Maybe bringing her was a bad idea. I didn't have time for introductions. I needed to find out what was going on.

"Why do I need *more* money?" I asked.

"For this," Mrs. Henry said, grabbing a piece of paper she had taped to her mirror and shoving it into my face.

It was a page out of some sort of beauty supply magazine, and what she'd circled in the middle looked like the queen of all hooded dryer chairs. Right under the picture was the sale price: $495.99.

"It's the Turbo Hoodie!" she said. "It has ten different heat settings, solid wood armrests, and *real* leather upholstery. It even has speakers so you can listen to music."

Her eyes were dancing. I'd never seen her so happy. "I would 'ave neva, been able to afford it before."

"But it basically costs 500 dollars, and I don't even have the 113 dollars I already owe you," I cried.

"Oh, but I think you will," she said smiling.

The bake-off! How'd she know?

"You and I both know yur gon' win that contest. And when you do, I'll be waitin' for my money." As she turned and walked away, I half expected her to start cackling like a witch. How did she know I was going to enter the contest? And why did she think I was going to win?

• • •

That night in the kitchen, I started gathering all my cake ingredients for the bake-off so my mom and dad could take them to the church. In a typical bake-off, you would just bake your cake at home and bring it for display and tasting at the contest. But, of course, with Mrs. LaRue running things, this bake-off would be anything but typical. Although most of the contestants would bake their cakes at home and bring them to the contest—the church only has three ovens—Mrs. LaRue had decided that in order to "spice things up," there needed to be some drama. So ten of the contestants would make their cakes live at the event. I was one of the "lucky" ten.

"I thought it was supposed to be a baking contest, not a reality show," Mom said as she helped me pack my stuff.

"Yeah, I know," I said. "But you have to admit, it kinda does make things more exciting."

Mrs. LaRue didn't know it, but my favorite reality show was *Ten-Minute Chef.* Every week it challenges chefs to use ten ingredients to create a meal in ten minutes. Talk about suspense! Although at the moment, *Ten-Minute Chef* had nothing on the reality that was my life.

Evonne had set everything up with Mason—again—for this Friday night. The plan was for me to sleep over at Evonne's and sneak into her backyard to meet Mason after her mom went to sleep. When she told him our idea, she said he smiled real hard, nodded, and said, "I didn't know she was like *that*."

She asked what he meant, and he told her "Don't worry about it." Evonne wasn't sure what he was talking about, but we weren't too worried about it. We just hoped he'd follow along. What Mason didn't know was that Leela and her girls would be hiding in the bushes—Leela insisted—to make sure I didn't wimp out. If everything went right, I'd kiss Mason, and collect my money from Leela after he left.

Evonne's mother was driving us directly to the church the next morning, so I needed to have everything ready to go tonight. I had to hurry, though—they would be here any minute.

"Everything OK, Gabby?" Mom asked.

"Sure, Mom," I lied. "Why?"

"You just haven't seemed like yourself lately.

That's because I haven't been.

"I'm fine, Mom. There's just a lot going with school. I have a big book report due on Monday, and an algebra test is coming up. You know how math stresses me out."

"Is the work starting to be too much?" she asked. "We're sending you there to get a good education, not get stressed out."

"No, I'll be fine," I said. What I really wanted to say was "Help!"

"Are you upset that Ma McGee can't make it?" asked Mom.

Before we even knew about the bake-off, Ma McGee had planned to visit Dad's little brother, Uncle Ray, to help him and Aunt Nicole with my new baby cousin. I was kinda bummed that she couldn't come, but I understood.

"No," I sighed. "I'm fine."

"Well, this wouldn't have anything to do with Mason Gambrell would it?" she asked.

"Huh?" I said.

"You heard me," she said. "I saw how you were acting in church last Sunday and at the mall. I think I know what's going on here."

What did she know? Was I about to be busted?

"Believe it or not, I was a girl once, too, Gabby," she continued. "And even though you think I'm ancient, I'm not too old to remember what it's like to like a boy."

I busied myself packing the ingredients while she went on.

"It can be a great feeling, but it can also be confusing," she said. "I mean, it's hard to know who's sincere. Mason seems nice and all, but he also seems kind of slick. You know, too cool for school."

Slick? Too cool for school? What was she talking about?

"Look, Mom," I said. "Mason's cute, but I don't like him, really."

"Really?" she asked skeptically.

"Really," I lied.

"Well, OK. You know, I'm glad we're going to that *Jill Jones* show," she said, changing the subject. "I know it doesn't seem like it, but I do like to see you have fun."

"I know, Mom," I said, unconvinced.

Handing me the raw sugar, she said, "I know we're strict with you, but there's so much going on in the world these days. There are so many things that can get you into trouble. And it's easy to get mixed up with the wrong kids. It's not like when I was growing up."

Maybe she *would* understand. I sure was tired of all these schemes and lies.

"Look, Mom, I . . ." I trailed off.

"Yes, Gabby?" Mom prodded.

Beep-beep! A loud honk from the driveway interrupted us. It was Evonne and her mom. I couldn't back out now. Evonne was right. Mom was too into her natural hair thing. She would never understand how I got myself into this.

"Is there something you need to tell me?" Mom asked.

"Uh, no, not really," I said, avoiding direct eye contact.

"You sure?"

"Yeah, I'm sure," I said with as much confidence as I could create.

Well, have a good time," Mom said, hugging me. "I'll finish packing up. You'll have everything you need at the church ready and waiting for you tomorrow morning, I promise."

I wanted to tell her the truth, but I just couldn't. The words just wouldn't come. She would be furious, and I would never get to see *Jill Jones*. Plus, I'd never live it down with Leela. So I did the only thing I could do. I hugged her back, gave her a kiss on the cheek, and headed out the door.

Ten

At first, Evonne and I were having so much fun that I forgot why we'd arranged the sleepover in the first place. Evonne's mom got a large pizza from Papa Pino's dripping with cheese and pepperoni, which we devoured as we watched *Jill Jones*. After the show, we turned to one of the music channels and I got to catch up on all the videos I didn't get to see at home. We laughed, sang, and tried to imitate the latest dance moves. Mrs. Edwards even joined in. Actually, she was having such a good time that I thought she would never go to bed.

Finally, at around 1:00 a.m., she claimed that she "couldn't hang" anymore and headed upstairs. As soon as she closed her bedroom door, Evonne hopped up, grabbed her phone, and started texting Mason.

"Wait!" I said.

"What?" asked Evonne.

I'm scared.

"Let's just wait just a few minutes," I said.

"Why?"

I'm terrified.

I looked around.

"Look, Gabby," Evonne pleaded. "The sooner I text Mason and Leela, the sooner we can get this thing over with. And I would like to be done with it as soon as possible. Your parents aren't the only ones who'll go crazy if they catch you with a boy. If my mom sees Mason here this late at night, she'll go off."

"That's what I mean," I said. "Don't you think we should wait until she's completely asleep?"

Biting her lip, Evonne agreed. "Yeah, you're right," she said, setting down her phone. "It shouldn't be long, though. My mom never stays up this late—and the good thing is that when she falls asleep, she's usually knocked out."

Evonne plopped down next to me on the couch.

"Well at least we got the hair thing right this time."

"Yeah," I said.

I didn't know it at the time, but Leela did me a favor by sabotaging us at the dance. After waiting in Lofton's over-heated locker room, my hair was a disaster. I would have been humiliated if Mason had seen me. This time, Evonne upped the heat on the flat iron and turned down the heat in their house. We were probably being silly and we were a little cold, but I didn't want to take any chances.

"Gab, I know you're nervous around Mason, but I'll be here the whole time," Evonne said. "Look, just pretend Mason is that guy you kissed at camp."

Ugh. The nonexistent kiss. I couldn't take it anymore. I don't know if it was all the sneaking around or what, but I started crying and explaining the whole thing. And you know what? It felt good.

Evonne hugged me. "Hey, we're best friends, right?"

"Right," I said.

"Well, that means you can tell me anything. I don't care if you've never kissed a boy," she said. "Guess what? Remember when I told you that I kissed Dougie Overton?

"You really didn't kiss him either?" I guessed.

"Oh, I kissed him," she said sheepishly. "It's just that it wasn't as great as I made it out to be. Actually, it was kind of gross because he had just eaten a hot dog and most of it was still stuck in his braces."

"Ewww," I squealed.

"Girl, by the time we got done, I felt like I had eaten it, too," she said, shuddering at the memory. "So, I haven't kissed anyone else yet. I'm waiting. Next time it has to be the best. With someone I *really* like.

"Like Derek?" I asked.

"Yeah, like Derek. Anyway, I think most kids make too big a deal out of it."

"Really?"

"Really," she said. "And you know what else? You don't have to do this. Let's call this whole thing off."

"I can't. You know I need the money. My mom will kill me if she finds out about all of this. Anyway, don't you want to see *Jill Jones?*"

"Well, yeah, but . . . are you sure?"

"I'm sure," I said more unsure than ever. "Your mom is probably asleep now. Go ahead. Get Leela over here, then text Mason."

After checking to make sure her mom was completely out of it, Evonne called Leela and told her to come over and wait behind the fence in the backyard. Then she waited ten minutes and texted Mason.

I played with my hair while we waited. It didn't feel as good this time. It was kind of stiff, and it smelled a little funny. It wasn't exactly run-your-fingers-through soft, but anything was better than the way it ended up looking at the dance.

Everyone lived around the corner, so Leela was here in a matter of minutes—and very soon after, Mason lightly tapped at the back door.

"Thanks for not making any noise," Evonne whispered to Mason.

"Hey, I don't want your moms to wake up, either," he said from the doorway. "Hey, Gabby."

"Hi," I said.

He looked so good. As he stood there grinning with his perfect teeth, the butterflies in my stomach started their dance. And cotton balls and sweaters started to show up, too. Still, Evonne was right. I was going to kiss the finest guy in Lofton—and get paid for it. Coat in hand, I was ready to head to the lighted patio out back. But Mason had other ideas. Before we knew what was going on, he was in the house!

"This is a nice house," he said, pushing past me. "I've never been up in here before."

What was he doing?

"Mason!" Evonne whispered urgently. "You and Gabby are supposed to see each other *outside.*"

"I know, but it's freezing out there," he said, walking around like he owned the place. "Oh, shoot, there's a basement."

With that, he bounded down the stairs before we could catch him. Evonne and I looked helplessly at each other. All of a sudden we heard Evonne's mother stirring upstairs.

"Evonne, y'all OK?" she asked from the top of the stairs.

"Yes, Mom," Evonne answered and then turned to me in a panic. "Look, I've got to go upstairs and make sure my mom doesn't come down. Get him OUT!"

"Alone?" I cried. "I can't."

"Just do it!" she whispered as she headed upstairs.

WWJJD (What would Jill Jones Do)? I tell you what she would do. She would march right down to the basement and take control of the situation. So, I took a deep breath, let it out, and went downstairs. When I got to the last step, I looked around. Evonne and I had spent many afternoons down here watching TV, and talking. I saw the familiar plush carpeting and comfy couch, but no Mason. I called out to him a couple of times, but he was nowhere. Where could he have gone? There was another entrance downstairs. Maybe he heard Evonne's mom and left. And maybe he got nervous and decided and this little "date" was over. With just the thought of that possibility, I felt my body relax for the first time that night. All of a sudden I heard, "Gotcha!" and someone grabbed me from behind. I shrieked but my mouth was covered. It was Mason. He had pulled me on to the couch and pinned me down.

Once my heart came out of my throat I asked, "What are you doing?"

"You should have seen your face!" he said, laughing hysterically.

My nervousness was quickly turning into a full-on panic. "OK, funny, ha-ha. We've got to go."

"Hey, your hair is different," he said.

"Yeah, Evonne did it," I said.

"What did she do? It smells burnt."

Burnt? I *knew* it smelled funny. Evonne had used too much heat.

"I was just trying something new," I said.

Seriously? I'm finally with Mason. Just us. Not a warden in sight. And we're talking about my hair. I couldn't *believe* we were discussing my hair.

"Oh," he said.

He finally got off of me and we both sat up. We were still really close, and I could smell his cologne. I had no idea what it was, but it smelled great. Leaning over, he started nuzzling my ear and I got warm all over. But this time it was nice. It was warm, not hot and uncomfortable like my "sweaters." Actually, I felt quite cozy and comfortable.

"Let's get down to it," he whispered.

Whoa, get down to it? I didn't like the sound of that.

"We've got to go outside like we planned," I said.

"It's too cold," he said taking off his jacket. "Besides, look around. We've got the whole basement to ourselves."

"No, you don't understand—"

"Sure I do," he said. "I know why I'm here."

That's when I realized that I was the one who didn't understand. Duh! I'd invited a boy—an almost fourteen-year-old boy—over to Evonne's house. At night. With no parents around. There was no telling what he was thinking. Although, I was starting to get a clue by the look in his eyes.

Suddenly, I heard something rustling around at one of the basement windows. I looked over Mason's shoulder. It was Leela! I had totally forgotten about her!

I could kiss him now, she would see it, and I could get my fifty dollars. But this was out of control and needed to end now. Plus, I realized that I didn't really know much about the person staring back at me, and he certainly knew nothing about me. I mean, he was cute and all, but the way he was looking at me made me feel really weird. I thought back to my conversation with Evonne. She was right. My first kiss should be everything. But this was nothing I wanted. A freezing basement, with burnt hair and "Leela & Friends" watching? For the first time, I didn't really care how slow I was. In fact, I could go on being the only unkissed seventh-grader in the world.

"Look, Mason, we've really got to go," I said, starting to get up.

"Why?" he asked, gently easing me back down to the couch. "Evonne's got everything under control. Come on girl, don't act like this isn't what you wanted."

All of a sudden, I heard footsteps coming downstairs. We were caught! Mason and I scrambled to our feet ready for the worst, but it wasn't Evonne's mom—it was Leela! In all the confusion, we must have left the door unlocked.

"Leela? What are *you* doing here?" Mason asked.

In that moment, even Leela looked confused—and very upset. She started to speak, and then we heard Evonne and her mom heading down from upstairs.

"Out there!" I said pointing to the basement door.

I didn't have to tell them twice. They were GONE.

Seconds later, Evonne and her mom were in the basement. "I could have sworn I heard something," Mrs. Edwards said.

"I told you it was nothing Mom," Evonne said. "Everything's fine."

Yeah, right. Everything was great.

Eleven

I woke up the next morning groggy from last night's disaster. Everything had gone wrong, but luckily for Evonne, her mom didn't suspect a thing. My luck, it seemed, had run out. With no money, I couldn't enter the contest. And no contest meant zero chance of paying back Mrs. Henry. And Mrs. Henry would definitely tell my mom, so I could forget about *Jill Jones*—and probably a lot of other things too.

"It's not so bad," Evonne said, trying to cheer me up as we got dressed. "We'll just go on watching her on TV like we always do."

"Yeah, I guess," I said.

"And I'll help you pay back Leela," she assured me.

"Uh-huh," I said, knowing that that was the least of my worries. I had to come clean to my folks before Mrs. Henry did. I figured I would tell them about everything after the bake-off. I had no idea what to say or where to start. My hair was out of sorts too. Half straight and half nappy, it didn't know what to do. Evonne offered to do it again, but I didn't feel like going through all of that so I brushed it back as much as I could and threw one of her bandannas over it.

Since I wasn't entering the contest, Evonne told her mom she'd run some errands with her. Evonne didn't want to be around for the fireworks with my mom, and I didn't blame her. So, they dropped me off at the church as everything was being set up. As I walked in and saw everything, I had to admit it. The BluBelles knew how to plan an event. There was lots of excitement in the air, and the church basement looked like something out of a glamorous movie set with flower arrangements, candles, and paintings. Not to mention the mayor's entourage and the Channel 7 television crew documenting everything. It looked great, but I couldn't believe Dad had agreed to all of this. He's definitely a less-is-more type of guy. My guess was that Mrs. LaRue had played the "charity card" throughout the planning for the bake-off and got Dad to say yes to pretty much everything. Spotting me as I came in, he rushed right over.

"Before you even say anything, I already know," he said. "It's too much."

"No, it looks great!" I said. "Maybe we should keep this new look."

"No way. This is Reed Street, not Hollywood," he said. "Did you register for the bake-off yet? You'd better start getting ready."

Dang! I guess I'd have to come clean sooner than I thought. "Dad, I—"

"Oh, shoot," Dad said interrupting me. "I see Mrs. LaRue. I've got to go. Hey, isn't that one of your friends from the neighborhood?"

I turned around to see Leela looking very, well, "un-Leela-like." For one thing, she had no makeup on and she was wearing sweatpants jeans and sneakers, which was a big difference from her usual miniskirts and skinny jeans. But the biggest change was that she seemed to look uneasy—not her usual cool self. Not at all like someone here to gloat and collect fifty dollars.

"Hey, Gabby," she said walking up to me. "I've been trying to track you down. Girl, you need to get a phone."

I rolled my eyes. "Look, Leela, I don't have the money on me now, I—"

"Actually, I'm here to pay up," she said, handing me fifty bucks!

I didn't get it.

"I figured I owe you," she said. "I was the one who interrupted you and Mason last night. I really never gave you a chance to finish the bet."

That was true, but I never expected that coming from her.

"Why *did* you do that?" I asked.

"Everybody knows I really like Mason," she said. "When I said that you should kiss him, I never thought that you would actually do it. When it looked like you would, I guess . . . well, I guess I just couldn't let it happen."

For the first time since I'd known her, Leela didn't look like she had it all together.

"Leela, I don't think Mason really likes me," I said.

"Really?"

"Really," I said. And I meant it.

"Look, thanks for the money," I said gratefully. "I really needed it."

"Yeah, I know. When I couldn't find you, I called Evonne and she told me everything. That's why I came down to the church. So you really *like* to bake? What's up with that?"

I didn't have time to explain. I had to get the money to Mrs. LaRue and get my stuff ready.

"Hey, I've got to go, but why don't you stick around? There will be lots of good stuff to eat soon."

"Cool. I'll stay for a little bit, but I'll need to leave in time to get ready for the game."

I'd totally forgotten about that! Today was the day Mason was going after Dad's scoring title. I couldn't believe it. Leela wasn't so bad after all. Maybe we could even be friends. Evonne was going to have a fit!

I rushed over to Mrs. LaRue to give her my newly found entry fee. As I approached, I could see that she was in a pretty intense discussion with my dad.

"Mrs. LaRue," Dad said. "Investing in our children's education is always a worthy cause, but I guess I'm just surprised and, well, disappointed to hear about where the BluBelles plan to donate the money."

"Well, I'm not sure why, Reverend McGee," Mrs. LaRue said. "Thornton Preparatory Academy is a wonderful school with a rich history, and I should know. I attended Thornton, and my daughter is in the seventh grade there."

"I know that Thornton Prep is a great school," Dad said. "My wife is an alumnus, and now Gabby goes there."

"Well, then, you should know that this is a worthy cause."

"Actually, I disagree. The last thing Thornton Prep needs is another library. You've done a great job of fundraising. Couldn't you at least give some of the money to one or two of the community charities that really need it? Like, the Helping Hands Homeless shelter or—"

"Or our soup kitchen!" I said.

"Please, Gabby, grown folks are talking here," Dad said.

"But it's true, Dad," I said. "Last week we had to turn away so many people that needed food."

"Reverend, I wish I could help, but I've already promised all of the money to the school," said Mrs. LaRue. "Look, I have to go, the mayor has just arrived. Gabby, I see you have your entry fee. I'll take that." She grabbed the money out of my hand and ran off in the direction of the mayor and his officials.

Dad turned to me looking upset.

"Gabby, I know you were trying to help, but what have I always told you about interrupting adult conversations?"

"I know. I'm sorry," I said. "I guess I just got riled up."

Dad's face eased up a bit. "Well, I guess I got a little riled up myself. Makes me glad that I did what I did."

"What did you do?" I asked.

"You'll see," he said with a smile. "Hey, I have to go take care of some things, and you've got to get ready to make the best cake ever, right?"

"Right, Dad. See you soon." I turned toward the kitchen with a thousand thoughts running through my head. What was Dad up to? Did Mom make sure to bring everything I asked for? Could I actually pull this off?

"Hey, watch it!" a voice said.

Once again, I guess I wasn't paying attention to where I was going and nearly ran into—Mrs. Henry! She was carrying a bunch of stuff and—hey!—she had cake stuff!

"Hi, Gabby," she said.

"Hi," I said, confused.

"Don't look so surprised, lil' girl. I can cook, too, you know. Plus, I could use the money."

I couldn't believe it—she was a contestant, too! I'd never even considered that she would enter, but I should have. Mrs. Henry was one of the church's better cooks. Plus, of course, she loves money. This woman was seriously evil. Having her in the contest could really hurt my chances, but it didn't matter to her. Why should it? If I won, she got her money from me; if someone else won, she got her money from my parents; and if she won, she got the money from the contest *and* my parents. For her, it was a win-win-win situation. The best I could do was break even. What I still couldn't figure out was how she knew I would even be in the bake-off when I'd only told my folks and Evonne.

• • •

The contest had started, and it seemed as if everyone in Lofton was there. I saw community leaders, residents, church members, the mayor, Channel 7, a sour-looking Camille, and even Headmaster Brookfield. Yup. Brooksie was at Reed Street. It was really weird. He looked the same, though—nose in the air, looking around for a kid to harass. But I didn't have time to think about him. Cake Girl had to get into serious baking mode. Since there were only three ovens, I had to get my cake in at my allotted baking time—11:30 a.m. As I started sifting my dry ingredients, I noticed Mrs. Henry on my right. When I saw her take out a jar of what looked like some type of coconut icing, my heart sank. Mrs. Henry's coconut-lemon iced pound cake was legendary at Reed Street. Folks liked to joke that her hair salon and pound cake were the only reasons people put up with her. But I couldn't give up now. Not when I was so close. I mean, wasn't it a sign that Leela showed up at the last minute with the fifty bucks I needed? Even though getting my hair done was a complete disaster and getting with Mason was a bust, I still had the chance to settle my debt with Mrs. Henry so she would keep quiet about my salon fiasco. That meant that I would still get to see the *Jill Jones* taping, and even more important, avoid my mom's wrath. So, I got to work.

The secret to a flawless cake? Well, it's not any one thing. It's more in the way you care for your cake. Like Ma McGee says, "Your cake is your baby, and you always have to care for your baby." And sometimes, it's just the little things that can make your baby happy. Like only using room-temperature eggs. Or, rotating your pans during baking. Even better, positioning your cake as close to the center as possible for maximum air circulation. But overall, you've got to bake with love. Ma McGee says if you love on your cake, everyone else will too. So I put in as much love as I could. And, as always, everything around me fell away while I was baking. Before I knew it, my six cake layers had cooled and were perfectly stacked, and I was spreading the fudgiest frosting I'd ever made all over them. For a moment as I looked my creation up and down, nothing else mattered. Not my crazy hair. Not my failed crush. Just six layers of chocolate perfection.

Bang!

"Sorry," another contestant yelled.

With the drop of a pan, I snapped back to reality. The contestants had been baking like mad, and the smells rising from the kitchen signaled that it would soon be time for the official taste test. A panel of five judges—including the mayor, my headmaster, and three local businesspeople—were evaluating the cakes based on presentation, difficulty, and, of course, taste. I was pretty confident about how my cake would hold up against everyone else's—except Mrs. Henry's. But before I had time to think about whether or not I'd added enough vanilla to my batter, the judging started. From the judges' smiles and nods, there wasn't a bad cake in the bunch. After about an hour of chewing and lip smacking, Mrs. LaRue had an announcement to make.

"Ladies and gentlemen, may I have your attention?" she said. "The judges have reached a decision. However, right now we invite all of you to sample all the entries to decide for yourself who *you* think the winner is. We'll be back soon to announce the results of the first annual BluBelles' Cake Bake-Off!"

Although everyone was anxious for a winner, they were also eager to taste the cakes, which were all delicious. Bunches of people were crowding the display tables and I noticed some of them as regulars from the soup kitchen! Something told me this had something to do with Dad's little surprise. When I found him, he was in yet another serious discussion with Mrs. LaRue.

"I don't understand, Mrs. LaRue. You told me that I was free to invite twenty special guests."

"I know, but the mayor's here, and this doesn't exactly look… well…good."

"I think it looks great," Dad said. "Like Gabby said, I was forced to turn a lot of these people away last week, and you have more than enough food here—too much food, in fact."

Way to go, Dad! I was so proud. But Mrs. LaRue was unmoved.

"I understand what you're trying to do, Reverend McGee, and it's a nice gesture, really it is—but this is neither the time nor the place."

Was she kidding? I wanted to scream that this was exactly the time and the place, but remembering what Dad said earlier about adults talking, I kept my mouth shut.

"Mrs. LaRue, this may be your event, but it's my church," Dad said. "I'm not asking these people to leave, and neither are you."

Go, Dad!

"Just watch me, Reverend," Mrs. LaRue said. With that, she turned and started trying to gather people. She focused in on a kid getting ready to try my cake. "Oh, young man, young man, I'm so sorry, but you're going to have to leave."

Mrs. LaRue's jaw dropped as the boy turned to face her. It was Derek Arrington with his family! Recovering quickly, she began explaining that he and all the folks that had just come in would have to go.

"I'm sorry, but this is a private event," she said. "I hope you understand. Didn't you all get the check we sent?"

"Yeah, we got it, but y'all are going to see it right back in your mailbox," Mr. Arrington said.

"Can't your family use the money?" Mrs. LaRue said.

"Sure, but we don't want a payoff."

"Payoff? What do you mean?"

By then, Mr. LaRue and Camille had made their way into the commotion.

"Come on, Vivian," Mr. LaRue said, grabbing his wife's arm. But Mrs. LaRue wasn't having it.

"What is he talking about, Miles?" she asked.

"Oh, you didn't know?" Mr. Arrington said. "Miles wants me to help keep his friend Howard out of jail by not testifying against him in the fraud investigation, but that's not going to happen."

"Fraud?! Look, we lost a good deal of money on that investment deal too," Mrs. LaRue said.

"Really? That's not how I heard it," Mr. Arrington said. "People are starting to say that Miles knew the deal was a scheme from the beginning, and his friend gave him a cut of the profits to lure people in. I'm sure the police will find that pretty interesting."

Mrs. LaRue turned toward her husband. "Miles, you said that this was all a misunderstanding. You said it would all be cleared up in no time."

"This isn't the time, Vivian," Mr. LaRue said angrily.

"Is that so?" Mrs. LaRue said. "Well, I'll bet we wouldn't even be standing here if it weren't for you. It all makes sense now. Everyone's been talking behind my back about you being a fraud. The folks at Evanswood wouldn't even look at me when they said we could no longer have the bake-off there, and The Crystal Cove never returned my calls but no one would tell me why. If it hadn't been for the other BluBelles, we wouldn't have even been able to host this event. You've ruined our reputations."

Camille, who had been avoiding eye contact with Derek, looked mortified. "Yeah, Daddy, I can't even get a hair appointment with André. And Mother was forced to go to Shear Wonders!" she said.

"Camille!" Mrs. LaRue spat out. "You weren't supposed to repeat that to anyone!"

That's how Mrs. Henry knew! Wow, Mrs. LaRue at Shear Wonders. I'm sure she paid extra money to clear out the shop so no one would see her. I guess Mrs. Henry figured I had a good chance of winning and, to better her chances of getting the money, she entered herself.

Clearly unmoved by the inconveniences experienced by his wife and daughter, Mr. LaRue looked at them like they each had two heads.

"Maybe if you two didn't spend so much, I wouldn't have to resort to using *creative* ways to make money," he yelled. And then, knowing he'd said too much, he stormed out of the church.

Camille started bawling, but Mrs. LaRue was so stunned she didn't seem to notice. Or maybe she just didn't care.

Suddenly, the mayor appeared right behind her.

"Vivian," he said, "I want to talk to you!"

"I know, Mayor Wilson," Mrs. LaRue said with her best the-show-must-go-on face. "But don't worry, I'll straighten everything out, and we can get on with the contest."

"Why?" he asked. "This is wonderful."

"It is?" she asked, looking confused.

"Of course!" he said. "Reverend McGee explained your special guests, and I'm very impressed."

Mrs. LaRue was looking crazy! "Well . . . I . . ."

"These days most people would rather turn their heads than take action when they see someone in need," Mayor Wilson continued. "So when Pastor McGee told me that you'd insisted on inviting the people he was forced to turn away from his soup kitchen last week, I thought it was an appropriate and timely gesture! I mean, you must know that increasing funding for the programs that help the homeless is one of the top things on my agenda for this year."

Mrs. LaRue was speechless. Speechless!

"In fact, I think I've figured out your surprise charity for the bake-off," he said. "Is it the Reed Street Church soup kitchen?"

"Why . . . yes," Mrs. LaRue stammered. "Yes, it is."

"I knew it!" he said. "This is great. Great cakes and great food for a great cause. Yes, well, I guess you'll be making the announcement soon. Don't worry, though. I won't say a word." After that, he was off, leaving Mrs. LaRue to deal. I couldn't believe it. Dad was the best.

"Mom, what's going to happen to *us*?" Camille asked.

Mrs. LaRue threw back her shoulders, smiled her brightest smile, and dived head first into denial. "Everything's going to be fine, Camille," she said, holding Camille's face in her hands. "Now just gather yourself and go sit down somewhere. I've got an event to host."

Mrs. LaRue marched off like she was going to pull a kid out of a burning building, Camille trailed after her, and Derek headed straight for me.

"Unbelievable!" he said, cracking up. "Looks like Mr. LaRue is in a lot of trouble."

"Yeah, but it was great!" I said. "Hey, how are you?"

"I'm doing OK. Things are getting better now," he answered. "I guess everyone knows everything by now, huh?"

"Yeah, and well . . . you know if there's anything—"

"I know," Derek said. "We've been kind of lying low. It's been tough, but my dad finally gets that we need some help, so we're going to move into my aunt's house for a while."

"Really? That's great. Why did you come here today, then?"

"Your dad asked us to. I guess he was teaching Mrs. LaRue a lesson. Actually, I've learned a lot, too. Especially about who my real friends are," he said as he watched Camille sulking in a chair. "I can't believe she won't even *look* at me."

"Yeah, well, personally I think you're better off."

"Yeah, I feel like a real fool, though. I thought she really liked me."

"Well, you've got plenty of other friends, and going back to Lofton won't be so bad."

"Yeah, I'll miss all the cool stuff at Thornton, but I'll be all right at Lofton. Even Hannah thinks so."

"Really?" I asked.

"Yeah. You know she's not like Camille, right? Just because she's rich doesn't mean she can't be a good friend."

Dad interrupted us. "Hey, it wasn't part of her plan, but I guess Mrs. LaRue got a few surprises today."

"It was great, Dad!" I said.

"Yeah, well I knew I was taking a chance asking all of these folks to come here."

"How did you know it would work out like that?"

"I didn't, Gabby," he said. "And, I had *no idea* about all the trouble caused by Mr. LaRue. But I do know that when you do what's right, you'll never go wrong."

That's when I knew I didn't deserve to win.

The loudspeaker came on. "Everyone, everyone— please, I need everyone's attention."

We turned around to see a cheery Mrs. LaRue up at the podium. I couldn't believe it. She looked happy and was practically glowing. Nothing like the defeated woman whose husband had stormed out of here just five minutes ago.

"It's time to announce the winner," she said. "But first—"

The audience groaned.

"But first, I would like to announce that all of the money from the first annual BluBelles' Cake Bake-Off is going to . . . the Reed Street Church soup kitchen!"

Everyone went wild. People couldn't believe it. And by looking at Headmaster Brookfield's dropped jaw I could tell he *really* couldn't believe it. Once the applause died down, Mrs. LaRue got to the real business at hand. "And now the winner. It was a tough choice, which—by the way—came very close to being a tie, but the winner of the first annual BluBelles' Cake Bake-Off is . . . Angelique Henry for her lemon-coconut pound cake!"

As I watched Mrs. Henry rush to the stage, I couldn't believe that the very person that caused me to have to go through all this craziness in the first place would end up helping me fail. As camera flashbulbs went off, Mrs. Henry was all smiles while accepting the trophy and the five-hundred-dollar check. I felt sick.

"Congratulations, Angelique," Mrs. LaRue said. "Please tell us, what is the secret to this great cake?"

"Well, I have the lemon-coconut icing flown straight from my mudda in Jamaica," she said, smiling proudly.

A few of the BluBelles gasped.

"So you didn't make the icing yourself?" a wide-eyed Mrs. LaRue asked.

"Well . . . no," Mrs. Henry said. "I would have, but it's a secret recipe from my mudda, and she won' tell anyone, not even family."

Now it was Mrs. LaRue's turn to be sick. "Well, I'm sorry to have to tell you this—especially in front of everyone—but the rules state that all entries *must* be made from scratch."

"Oh, but it was," Mrs. Henry said.

"Yes, but not by you," Mrs. LaRue explained. "It must be made from scratch by the contestant."

More flashbulbs went off, and everyone started whispering. The Channel 7 reporter who'd earlier looked bored and irritated perked up as though he had stumbled across a presidential scandal.

Flustered and embarrassed, Mrs. Henry tried to explain. "Oh, I . . . it was just the icing . . . I didn't think—"

"I understand, but rules are rules," Mrs. LaRue said. "So I guess that makes Gabby McGee the winner."

I couldn't believe it. I'd won. After everything I'd gone through, I should have been ecstatic—but I wasn't. For some reason I just felt weird. I mean, it was all so wrong. *At every turn, I'd made the wrong choice*, I thought as I passed an angry Mrs. Henry on the way up to the podium to accept my trophy and check from Mrs. LaRue.

"I assume your cake was made exclusively by you, right Gabby?" Mrs. LaRue asked wearily.

"Oh, yeah, of course," I said.

"Great. Well, then, I'll just ask: Do you have any special plans for your prize money?"

And, for the very first time since this whole thing started, everything became clear.

Twelve

You win some, you lose some. I didn't have to pay back Mrs. Henry, but the closest I would ever get to *Jill Jones* would be through our flat-panel TV—and that wouldn't be for a very long time.

After I won the prize, I announced that I would be donating all of the money to the soup kitchen. Everything that was going on with Derek made me realize that the things that I thought were a big deal, weren't. First off, changing my hair just because that's what everyone else was doing was silly. Plus, it looked painful. Of course, I still had issues with my hair, but I was starting to wonder why I didn't think my own hair wasn't good enough. Maybe I needed to figure that out before I made any big changes to it. Secondly, Mason Gambrell was clearly out of my league. Not that he was better than me, but he's definitely ready for some things that I'm not. Of course, I still dreamed of feeling the way that other girls did when they first kissed a boy, but now I knew I would be OK if I waited a little longer. Actually, looking at how miserable Leela looked last night made me see that boys could really complicate your life.

Anyway, everyone was glad that I decided to give the money to the soup kitchen. Everyone, that is, but Mrs.

Henry. Once I stepped away from the podium she was waiting for me.

"Well, lil' girl, what we gon' do now?" asked a furious Mrs. Henry. "What about my money?"

"What money?" asked my mom, who'd come to congratulate me.

Mrs. Henry spun around to Mom and spilled everything. She was just too happy to tell her everything that had gone down at the salon. Mom was mad, but she couldn't go off now, not at the church. Still, she wasn't about to let this go. I thought she was about to tell me to head home so she could give me the "Cousin Bobby" treatment, but she started in on Mrs. Henry!

"Look, Angelique," she said, "Gabby was wrong for coming to the salon without my permission, but we both know she didn't break your already brokedown hair dryer."

"Den why when she ran into it, did it just stop workin'?" she cried in front of a growing crowd of ladies.

"Angelique, those dryers haven't changed since I've been getting my hair done there, and you've been doing my hair for almost twenty years!" Mrs. Nixon chimed in.

"Yeah," Mrs. Patterson said. "And didn't I hear you bragging last month about how you had ordered three of the latest and greatest top-of-the-line hair dryers?"

"Uh-huh," Ms. Chatham chimed in. "You said the ones you had were on their last legs, and you wouldn't be surprised if they quit on you any day now."

"That's right," Mrs. Patterson added. "She said she had most of the money and just needed to figure out how to pay for one more."

I couldn't believe it! Mrs. Henry had lied. Even worse, she'd tried to con a twelve-year-old out of five hundred dollars. Mom looked disgusted.

"I can't believe you, Angelique," she said. "I mean, I knew you were cheap, but this is bad even for you. And Gabby, you *really* know better! Well, it looks like there's been enough bad behavior to go around here, and I think I know how we can fix *everything*."

Mrs. Henry and I didn't like the look in Mom's eyes.

Even though we'd discovered that I really didn't owe Mrs. Henry any money, Mom said that as part of my punishment for sneaking around behind her back, I would be working at Mrs. Henry's hair salon for a couple of hours after school one day a week and one Saturday a month. Plus, Mom thought it was a good idea for Mrs. Henry to provide free hair services to all the homeless women at the local shelter who were trying to find work. Not giving Mrs. Henry much of a choice, she announced it right away to the crowd. FREE hairstyling! I thought Mrs. Henry would pass out right there!

After that, the Channel 7 news reporter announced that between the bake-off and all the donations to the homeless, he was certain he'd get a prime spot on that evening's six-o'clock news, and that made everyone—including Mrs. Henry—happy. I just couldn't believe that despite all that had gone wrong, everything had turned out great. Well, almost everything. In addition to being Mrs. Henry's slave, my mom took me aside to let me know that there was no way I would be going to see *Jill Jones*.

"You do know that going to the *Jill Jones* taping is out now. Right?" Mom said.

"Yeah, I know," I said with a nod, my heart racing.

"I'm pretty mad about all the lying, Gabby," she continued. "And I'm almost just as upset about the reason you felt you had to lie. Is having straight hair *that* important?"

"I know it seems silly to you, but I don't know, I just feel like my hair looks crazy."

"I realize that fitting in seems crucial to you at your age," she said. "And pretty soon you'll be making your own decisions about how you want your hair—and you may get a relaxer. I guess I just always hoped that your own hair would be good enough. I hated my hair almost my whole life because I was trying to conform to someone else's standard of beauty, but that may not make sense to you right now."

"Well, to be honest, I'm still not sure about the whole 'good hair/bad hair' thing, so I think I can wait on getting a relaxer—for now. In the meantime, maybe I can at least get it pressed?"

She smiled. "Well, we'll see. But maybe what I can do is take a break from being a hairdresser and we can try getting our hair done by someone who actually knows what they're doing."

"Really, Mom?" I asked.

"Really," she said, hugging me.

"I guess Mrs. Henry would be willing to do our hair now that everything has worked out," I said.

"Actually, I saw a new natural hair salon at the mall I want to try," she said.

Just as I started getting excited about that possibility, Dad came over.

• • •

Dad was pretty hot when he found out about everything. He told me to come with him and I was sure he was taking me straight home to warm up my behind, but after we got in the car and he headed in the opposite direction of our house toward town, I realized we were headed for Lofton Middle. He really wanted to get at me for the trouble I'd caused, but he also really wanted to catch the last period of the game. So he pretty much went off on me for the whole ride over, especially after I filled him in on everything else—including the bet and inviting Mason over to Evonne's house. He reminded me that lying was never an answer to a problem, that I could come to them about *anything*, and boys were off limits until I was sixteen.

We got there in record time, and we could see from the parking lot that the gym was packed. Everything was on the line tonight. Lofton's chances to compete for the state championship *and* Dad's scoring title, which would probably be Mason's title after tonight. But after getting there and hustling into the gym, we were shocked. Lofton was only up by one point! The score was 55 to 54, and Thornton Prep had just gotten the ball. I couldn't believe that the Thornton team was actually hanging in there with Lofton. Even more surprising was the surge of pride I felt for my school. I saw Hannah and a small group of Thornton students and parents by the Thornton bench. They all looked so happy.

There were no seats left so we stood by the door and tried our best to see the game through the crowd. Steven West from Thornton dribbled down the court for an easy layup, and Mason fouled him hard. Ouch! Mason was much bigger than Steven—and bigger than just about everyone else out on the court—so I knew Steven had to be hurting. But, as Dad explained, it was actually a good thing for Thornton, because it meant he could shoot two free throws. All the Lofton fans—who occupied most of the gym—were waving, yelling, and doing their best to try to distract Steven. Even Dad got in on it. Even though Dad didn't want to lose his scoring title, he still wanted Lofton to win. Strangely enough, I was kind of rooting for Thornton to pull an upset.

Swish! Steven drained the first one. The score was tied! The gym got even louder. Kids, teachers, and parents were doing everything they could to stop the next ball from going in. Steven dribbled, looked up, took a deep breath, and launched the ball. It hit the rim, bounced, and went in! Thornton was up now, 56 to 55!

The Lofton fans all groaned in unison. But with ten seconds left on the clock, Lofton had the ball and everyone started chanting, "Lofton . . . Lofton . . . Lofton."

"Ten seconds—plenty of time for Lofton to score and Mason to claim the scoring title," Dad yelled.

He was right. Although Mason had been held to only five points, a basket would put Lofton *and* him over the top. As Mason dribbled up the court, the crowd started the countdown.

"Ten!"

Mason was immediately covered by two Thornton players.

"Nine!"

He looked to his left for help but there was no one.

"Eight!"

Then he looked to his right.

"Seven!"

Suddenly, DaShawn broke open for an easy shot!

"Six!"

Mason was still hanging on to the ball.

"Five!"

Mason was still looking to take the shot himself!

"Four!"

"Pass it to DaShawn! He's wide open!" Coach Sterling screamed.

"Three!"

Mason still hung on to the ball as Thornton defenders surrounded him.

"For Pete's sake, Mason, throw DaShawn the ball!" Coach Sterling yelled.

"Two!"

What was he doing?

"One!"

Just as the last second ran out, Mason launched the ball toward the basket. It seemed to take forever as we watched the fate of Lofton's season and the single-season scoring record travel with the ball.

Clank! It hit the back of the rim and bounced up over the backboard. *Buzzz!* The game was over. We were all in shock.

As the folks filed down from the bleachers, no one could believe it. Especially the Lofton players, who were still on the court.

"I was wide open, man!" DaShawn yelled at Mason.

"Look, I had to take the shot," Mason said. "It was for the season, man."

"Yeah . . . our season or *yours?*" DaShawn said, walking off.

Everyone knew that Mason had put himself before the team, and he got an earful from the coach, his teammates, and a lot of folks in the stands.

Thornton Prep, on the other hand, was ecstatic. Although they never had any chance of getting in the state tournament, as far as they were concerned, this *was* their state championship—and they had won. Dad spotted an excited Hannah in the stands and waved. As she started walking toward us, I tried to figure out what to say. I was such a jerk the last time we talked.

"Looks like you cheered Thornton to victory," Dad told Hannah.

"Yeah, I knew they could do it," she said. "I guess you're kind of disappointed, though."

Dad chuckled. "Yeah, a little, but the best team won. Hey, girls, I see an old buddy I want to say 'hi' to. Gabby, why don't you meet me out front. Good to see you again, Hannah."

Once Dad left I still didn't know what to say, but I had to make it right.

"Well, I guess I was wrong about Lofton beating Thornton," I said with a sigh.

"*And?*" Hannah said, smiling and obviously enjoying my discomfort.

"And I was wrong about you. You're not like Camille," I said. "In fact, you're nothing like Camille. Except for having an obscene amount of money."

She laughed.

"Really, Hannah, I'm sorry," I said. "I guess it really made me mad when you kept defending Camille."

Hannah smiled. "Well, I guess I was wrong, too. About Camille, I mean. She's really pretty shallow. I guess I just wanted to think she was better than that."

I thought about everything that happened at the bake-off. "Well, maybe she'll come around. You never know what might force someone to change for the better."

Hannah looked surprised *and* confused, but unfortunately, I had no time to explain. I spied my dad heading for the front door and waving for me to join him. My official grounding had begun. I told her I'd fill her in at school on Monday and left quickly to meet Dad.

"Well, at least you still have your record," I said as we walked to the car.

"Yeah, you're right, I do," he said, brightening. "I was getting kind of sad at the thought of it going down. With Mason headed to high school next year, I think it will be a long time before anyone else can challenge it. Mason is a one-of-a-kind player."

"I guess, but he really isn't that great of a person," I said.

"Yeah, well, everyone makes mistakes," he said. "I'm sure a lot of the points I scored back then came at the expense of some of my teammates. To tell the truth, I *was* a bit of a ball hog."

"Really?" I asked. Somehow, I just couldn't picture my father—the pastor—as a ball hog.

"Yeah," he said with a laugh. "Otherwise, I don't think I would have scored as many points as I did. Anyway, Mason's still young. He has plenty of growing up to do. Kind of like you."

"Yeah," I said, knowing that Dad was right. Fortunately, I was starting to see that I shouldn't be in such a big hurry to do it.

Adrienne Vincent Sutton received her BA in English from Penn State University and went on to work in various writing and editing positions in publishing, marketing, and advertising. Currently living in the Baltimore, Maryland area, with her husband and two daughters, she started writing fiction in her spare time. *Bad Hair Day* is her first novel. To learn more about her, visit adriennevincentsutton.com.

Made in the USA
Lexington, KY
15 May 2019